FORBIDDEN HEARTS

A Mafia Romance Bound by
Love, Sealed in Loyalty

Nolan Crest

Copyright © 2025 Nolan Crest

All rights reserved

The characters and events portrayed in this book are fictitious. Any similarity to real persons, living or dead, is coincidental and not intended by the author.

No part of this book may be reproduced, or stored in a retrieval system, or transmitted in any form or by any means, electronic, mechanical, photocopying, recording, or otherwise, without express written permission of the publisher.

Cover design by: Emily Harper
First Edition : 2025
Printed in the United States of America

Dedication

*For the ones who love like it's war—
bloody, beautiful, and worth every scar.
And for those who dared to choose love
in a world that taught them not to.*

"And what is hell? I maintain that it is the suffering of being unable to love."

FYODOR DOSTOEVSKY

CONTENTS

Title Page
Copyright
Dedication
Epigraph
Author's Note · 1
Preface · 3
Prologue · 4
Chapter 1 · 7
Chapter 2 · 15
Chapter 3 · 20
Chapter 4 · 26
Chapter 5 · 34
Chapter 6 · 40
Chapter 7 · 47
Chapter 8 · 52
Chapter 9 · 58
Chapter 10 · 64
Chapter 11 · 71
Chapter 12 · 77
Chapter 13 · 82
Chapter 14 · 90

Chapter 15	97
Chapter 16	102
Chapter 17	108
Chapter 18	113
Chapter 19	120
Chapter 20	129
Chapter 21	135
Chapter 22	140
Chapter 23	146
Chapter 24	152
Chapter 25	157
Chapter 26	163
Chapter 27	168
Chapter 28	173
Chapter 29	180
Chapter 30	184
Chapter 31	188
Chapter 32	195
Chapter 33	200
Afterword	204
About The Author	207
Books In This Series	209
Books By This Author	211

AUTHOR'S NOTE

Dear Reader,

This story is a symphony of contradictions—beauty laced with brutality, love stitched into violence, and hope blooming from ashes.

Forbidden Hearts was born not from a single idea, but from a thousand emotions—rage, longing, grief, desire—and the question that haunted me the most:

What happens when love dares to bloom between two people born to destroy each other?

Alessio and Isabella came to me not as perfect heroes, but as fractured souls shaped by bloodlines and betrayal. They are sharp edges and soft glances, bullets and poetry. And like all great love stories… they were never meant to be easy.

This is a tale of forbidden desire and war-born passion, but underneath it all—it's about choice. About fighting for the love the world says you cannot have, even when it costs everything.

If your heart breaks, if your breath catches, if you curse me as you turn the final page—know that I wrote this for you. For the reader who craves not just a romance, but a *reckoning*.

Thank you for letting me break your heart… and maybe, piece it back together.

With all my fire,

Nolan Crest

PREFACE

They say love and war cannot coexist.

But what happens when they are born from the same flame?

In a world where loyalty is everything and betrayal is a death sentence, two heirs of rival mafia empires are thrown into a collision course of passion, vengeance, and impossible choices.

Alessio Moretti is the dark prince of the Italian underworld—feared, ruthless, and bound by duty.
Isabella Romano is a rose among thorns—sharp-tongued, guarded, and promised to another for the sake of peace.

Their story is not one of instant love or easy redemption. It is slow-burn and steel-cut. It is stolen glances in enemy halls, whispered threats that sound like confessions, and kisses that taste like damnation.

Forbidden Hearts is a journey through the darkest corridors of the soul—where love is war, trust is dangerous, and survival is never guaranteed.

This is not a fairytale.

This is a love story carved from blood, lust, and the ghosts of legacy.

And once you enter… there is no turning back.

PROLOGUE

- Bloodlines -

THE DAY ALESSIO MORETTI watched his father die, the sun never touched his skin again.

It had been one of those rare days when the world felt still. Peaceful, almost deceitfully so.

Sixteen-year-old Alessio walked beside his father through the narrow streets of Palermo, sunlight slanting between worn terracotta roofs.

Don Lorenzo Moretti—feared, revered, untouchable—was laughing, his deep baritone echoing off the stones like thunder with no storm.

They sat on the edge of the marina, two shadows disguised as a father and son, sharing stolen moments and pistachio gelato. Lorenzo spoke of futures that would never come. He spoke of loyalty, of power, and of legacy—his words laced with love and iron.

"One day, *figlio mio*, you'll lead not with fear, but with fire," Lorenzo said, wiping the cream from his beard. "And they'll follow you not because they must… but because they should."

It was the last time Alessio would hear his father laugh.

They never saw the second car.

One moment: street chatter, clinking gelato spoons, and soft sea wind.

The next: an eruption of white heat, the world screaming in flame.

The explosion tore through the marina like a demon unchained. Alessio flew through the air—a ragdoll spun by fate—and landed hard on burning cobblestones.

Smoke poured into his lungs. His body broken. His skin shredded.

And beside him, there was nothing left of his father but a melting watch and a scorched family medallion.

"*Papà...*" he whispered, reaching out to empty space.

Men in suits pulled him from the wreckage. Their faces were blurs—some loyal, others not. The whispers began that same night: *It was the Romanos.*

Whether it was true didn't matter. It was enough.

Night fell, and with it, the last remnants of Alessio's innocence.

Wrapped in bandages, bruises blooming across his ribs, he stood in front of his father's coffin. His uncle—Don Salvatore—knelt beside him, one hand gripping his shoulder.

"You're a Moretti now," Salvatore said. "The blood doesn't make you. The *fire* does. And you, ragazzo… you were forged tonight."

Alessio stared down at the scorched medallion in his palm. His fingers tightened around it until they bled.

"I'll burn them all," he said, voice steel-flat. "I'll make them choke on their power. Every Roman—every traitor—every soul who smiled while he died."

And in that moment, the child died. The heir was born.

Not with a crown.
Not with applause.
But with fire in his eyes and a body count in his shadow.

And in the ashes, he made a vow that would outlive kingdoms:
The Romanos will pay.

CHAPTER 1

- The Offer -

ISABELLA ROMANO HAD never tasted freedom, but she imagined it tasted nothing like the wine her father poured.

Her eyes opened to morning light slanting through gauzy curtains, gold spilling over velvet like a lie. The bedroom smelled like roses—always roses.

Arranged in porcelain vases, hanging in woven garlands above the carved bedposts, infused into her perfumes and bathwater until she could no longer tell where her skin ended and their scent began.

But beneath the sugar of them was something else.

Rot.

Decay.

A sweetness that turned the stomach.

She sat up slowly, brushing her hair off her bare shoulder, her silk nightgown catching the light. Somewhere below, the iron gates groaned open, and the sound of men's voices floated through the estate like fog—sharp, commanding, territorial.

The wolves were already pacing.

And Isabella? She was the dove in a gilded cage, her wings clipped before they'd ever known the wind.

A soft knock.

"Miss Romano," came Mariella's voice—her lady's maid and the only person in this house who ever used the word 'please.' "Your father is waiting in his office."

Of course he was.

Don Emilio Romano never summoned unless it was to command. Isabella rose with the grace of someone born under a microscope, every step toward the wardrobe rehearsed, every movement exact.

The dress laid out was deep burgundy—blood-colored silk that clung like second skin.

She didn't pick it. She never did. And still, it fit perfectly.

Like every prison ever built for her.

The corridor leading to her father's study was cold despite the Sicilian heat. Ancient oil paintings lined the walls—portraits of grim-faced Romanos, eyes like wolves, mouths like blades.

Their judgment was eternal, and it weighed heavily every time she walked this path.

She didn't knock. She never did.

Don Emilio sat behind his massive mahogany desk, his dark eyes fixed on a crystal decanter as he poured two fingers of wine—black, bitter, ceremonial. He didn't look up.

"Sit."

She obeyed, spine straight, chin lifted.

"I'm not in the mood for theater, *papà*."

"Good. Neither am I." He took a slow sip. "Marco Bellini has asked for your hand."

The air in the room shifted—stilled.

Isabella blinked once. "You mean, *you've given* it."

He set the glass down with a soft *clink*. "You will marry him in three weeks."

She laughed—a sharp, venom-laced sound that echoed against the stone.

"Is that the joke? That I get a say?"

His gaze hardened. "You'll marry him because it brings peace. Because the Bellinis are useful. Because this alliance cements a power you could never understand."

Her hands curled into fists in her lap.

"I am not a pawn."

"No," he said quietly, rising from the chair. "You're the queen. And queens are sacrificed so kings survive."

He stepped around the desk, slow and deliberate, until he stood over her. A father in title. A tyrant in truth.

"You'll wear the dress. You'll smile. And when the time comes, you'll open your arms and your legs and do your duty like a good Romano."

Her breath caught.

But her voice—when it came—was ice.

"If you think I will lie down and pretend, you've mistaken me for mother."

His hand lashed out—not to strike, but to grab her chin, fingers digging into the bone.

"Don't you ever speak her name like that," he hissed.

"You are nothing without this family. Don't forget that."

She yanked away, her eyes flashing.

"Then maybe it's time you feared what I am with it."

He stared at her for a long moment. Then he turned, walked back to his desk, and refilled his glass.

"The Bellinis arrive tonight. There will be a dinner. And a representative from the Morettis will join us."

Isabella's blood went cold.

"The Morettis?"

"A show of peace," he said flatly. "You'll behave."

"You expect me to dine with men who've slaughtered ours in alleys?"

"I expect you to survive. Because that is what we do."

Her jaw clenched so tight she tasted blood.

The Devil's Dinner

THE DINING ROOM HAD been transformed into a theater of power—one where every smile was sharpened, every gesture rehearsed for an audience of enemies dressed as allies.

The table stretched long and gleaming beneath an antique chandelier dripping with crystal. Gold-rimmed china and engraved cutlery sparkled under the soft light.

The aroma of roasted meats, truffle risotto, and aged wine hung heavy in the air, yet none of it could mask the deeper scent beneath—the coppery edge of strategy, of betrayal, of old blood never fully washed away.

Isabella walked in last, by design.

Dressed in a deep emerald gown that kissed every curve and left her shoulders bare, she moved like smoke—deliberate, silent, untouchable. Her hair fell in elegant waves down her back, and her lips were stained the color of spiced wine.

The whole room turned to look at her, but she was looking only for one thing.

Or rather, one absence.

He wasn't here yet.

Good.

Marco Bellini—her soon-to-be fiancé by decree, not desire—rose and pulled her chair out as if he were some gentleman from a fairytale, not the spoiled bastard of a second-tier crime family.

He kissed her cheek, and she barely masked the way her skin crawled.

"You look ravishing tonight," he murmured, eyes lingering far too low. "Like sin wrapped in silk."

"Careful," she said, taking her seat. "You might choke on it."

He chuckled, not realizing her smile wasn't real.

Her father took his place at the head of the table, wearing his usual mask of solemn elegance. To his right sat the Bellinis. To his left, an empty seat waited.

Their guest had yet to arrive.

She took her wine glass—one of the rare indulgences she was allowed without consequence—and sipped it slowly, letting the bitterness settle on her tongue. As conversation resumed around her—idle talks of port expansions, whispered rumors of a shifting power in Naples—Isabella felt it like a storm pressing against her spine.

He was coming.

And when the door finally opened, it wasn't thunder that entered the room.

It was something colder.

Something darker.

Alessio Moretti.

He stepped into the dining hall with the poise of a king and the silence of a ghost. Time itself faltered around him. Conversations ceased. Forks stilled. Even her father straightened his shoulders.

He was taller now—broad-shouldered, sharp-jawed, dressed in obsidian black. No tie. No emotion. Just presence.

His hair was slightly tousled, his skin kissed by war, and his eyes—God, those eyes—were dark and endless, like two windows into the fire that had forged him.

He didn't smile.

He didn't bow.

He simply looked around the table like a predator studying prey.

And then his gaze locked with hers.

Isabella.

A breath she didn't know she'd been holding caught in her throat.

There was no recognition in his expression, yet every inch of her felt seen. Exposed. Dismantled.

He looked at her like she was not a woman... but a warning.

And she—she hated that her skin tingled.

That her pulse betrayed her.

That something deep inside her twisted, not in fear, but in defiance.

And desire.

Her father stood to greet him with the kind of tight smile that didn't reach the eyes. "Alessio," he said. "Welcome to Casa Romano. We hope this dinner marks a new era."

Alessio tilted his head slightly. "That depends on what's being served."

Don Emilio chuckled. "Peace."

"A bitter dish," Alessio murmured.

He took the empty seat beside Isabella.

Their elbows nearly touched. Their knees almost brushed. And when the server poured him a glass of wine, Alessio didn't touch it.

Instead, he leaned slightly toward her.

"Romano," he said, his voice low and gravel-warm, laced with something ancient and unreadable. "Did your father choose the wine? Or do you like things that burn going down?"

She didn't flinch. Didn't look away.

"I like things that bite," she replied. "Not ones that beg."

The tension between them sharpened.

And then—he smiled. Just barely. Just enough.

She felt the ground shift beneath her.

Her father had whispered it earlier, like an order dressed as advice: *"You'll smile when he walks in... even if it kills you."*

And now, as Alessio sat beside her—eyes flickering with something cruel and curious—her lips curved into a perfect, practiced smile.

But inside, she was burning.

Because this was the man she'd been raised to hate.

The ghost her family feared. The heir of fire. The bloodmarked boy who survived the inferno she'd heard about in hushed, forbidden stories.

This was Alessio Moretti.

And when their eyes met again, something unspeakable passed between them.

Not recognition.

Not even hatred.

Something older.

Something inevitable.

And then he walked in. Alessio Moretti.
And nothing—nothing—would ever be the same again.

CHAPTER 2

- Ghosts of Fire -

ALESSIO WORE A SUIT of silk, but beneath it, his bones itched for blood.

The Romano estate loomed ahead—gold-lit, opulent, drenched in the kind of wealth that reeked of old crime. He stepped from the armored car, the gravel crunching beneath his shoes like bones breaking beneath a boot.

Around him, his men remained still—silent, shadows at his back—but this wasn't a mission for numbers.

This was personal.

The iron gates of Casa Romano hadn't opened to a Moretti in nearly a decade.

Not since the fire. Not since the explosion that tore through his childhood and left him bloodied, gasping, clutching a medallion burned into his palm and a father's laugh turned into smoke.

They didn't know he remembered.

They didn't know he *knew*.

Not all of it—no. But enough.

Enough to smile politely at Don Emilio across a dining table while envisioning what his blood would look like against white marble floors.

Alessio adjusted his cufflinks, straightened his spine, and walked up the stone steps like a king returning to his stolen throne.

Every step was a grave he was willing to dig.

The Princess and the Predator

He smelled her before he saw her—jasmine, leather, and defiance.

She moved like heat over polished tile, and when she entered the dining room, silence followed her like a lover. Her gown was green, rich as envy, the slit high enough to kill a man where he sat.

She didn't smile—she *commanded*, and yet every move was controlled, rehearsed, political.

Isabella Romano.

He'd expected porcelain. He got steel wrapped in silk.

Her eyes met his—hazel, flecked with gold, ringed in something dark. Not innocence. Not naiveté.

Caution. Intelligence. Fire.

She didn't look away.

Neither did he.

The first thing he noticed was that she didn't flinch. Not like the others did when they saw him. There was no polite fear, no false flattery. Just this… standoff in silence, as if she were daring him to blink first.

The predator in him stirred.

She was dangerous.

He liked dangerous.

He sat beside her, their chairs so close the edge of her dress brushed his leg. She didn't shift away. He didn't apologize.

Instead, he leaned in slightly, just enough for her to smell the hint of smoke and leather on his suit.

"Romano," he said low, like a secret or a threat. "Do you always dress like a weapon, or is this for me?"

Her lips curved—barely. "Do you always arrive uninvited, or did my father beg for your presence?"

He laughed, soft and cold.

Touché.

He watched her throughout the meal. Not in the way a man watches a woman, but in the way a soldier watches an opponent. Studying tells. Reading strategy. Calculating weaknesses.

And yet—

He found none.

Only edges.

Only temptation.

Only a war worth starting.

Later, when the meal was done and the night had cooled into something deceptively quiet, Alessio found himself walking the Romano grounds alone—out of choice, not comfort.

He needed space. Distance.

Because something was wrong.

She was wrong.

He had prepared for this.

Had imagined this night for years.

The plan was clear: charm the table, earn trust, get close, find the cracks, exploit the truth, and when the time came—burn them all from the inside out.

But she was not part of that plan.

Not the way she looked at him.

Not the way she sounded—mocking but magnetic.

Not the way her voice slithered under his skin and made him remember he still had nerve endings left to burn.

His mind screamed vengeance.

His body whispered sin.

And he hated himself for it.

He paused at the edge of the rose garden, inhaling the scent of thorns, recalling blood.

"Lost?" came a voice behind him.

He didn't turn.

"I don't get lost," he said.

Isabella moved beside him, just close enough to graze.

Her arms were bare now. Her eyes were unguarded. For a second, she wasn't the princess. Just a girl in moonlight, as angry and ruined as he was.

"Then what are you doing out here?"

He turned toward her slowly. "Looking for the grave where your family buried the truth."

She raised a brow. "You'll need more than charm for that, Moretti."

"I wasn't planning on using charm."

A pause.

Then she stepped forward, her face inches from his.

"You're not the only one wearing a mask tonight."

And then she walked away.

Leaving behind jasmine, smoke, and something dangerously unfinished.

He watched her disappear into the shadows of her family's palace, back straight, chin high, every inch the enemy he had vowed to destroy.

He had come here for vengeance.

To tear the Romanos down brick by bloodstained brick.

But he hadn't planned on *her*.

CHAPTER 3

- Dance With the Devil -

SHE WORE BLACK because mourning her freedom felt appropriate.

Not that anyone here would notice. Not in a ballroom drowning in chandeliers, lace, and lies.

The Romano Annual Masquerade was a gilded spectacle—velvet and violin, marble and menace. It was tradition, a show of wealth and status masked behind smiles and champagne.

But for Isabella, it felt like a parade of cages—one more evening where she was dolled up, displayed, and dressed for someone else's narrative.

Tonight's dress was a masterpiece of manipulation. Fitted, strapless, with a slit that sliced dangerously up one thigh and a train that whispered power across the floor.

It had been hand-selected by her stepmother, tailored by someone who clearly didn't believe in subtlety, and paired with black silk gloves that reached her elbows.

She looked every inch the perfect pawn.

And she hated it.

Around her, masked guests danced and laughed, men in tailored suits exchanged veiled threats under the guise of diplomacy, and women in glittering gowns sold secrets with their smiles. Politics, after all, was just another waltz.

She sipped her wine, red and dry as her patience, and let her eyes sweep across the ballroom.

Her fiancé—*the ever-charming Marco Bellini*—was too busy boasting with a cluster of half-drunk heirs to notice she hadn't smiled in an hour. Perfect.

Let him rot in his own ego.

But the moment her father raised a single finger from the balcony above, she knew her role wasn't optional tonight.

"Alessio Moretti has arrived," Don Emilio said, voice cool, unreadable.

Of course he had.

She watched the room tilt, ever so slightly, as the name whispered through the crowd like smoke. Power arrived silently. Like a storm.

And when she turned, she saw him.

The Dance

He was dressed in black—of course—with no mask. Just a suit that fit like armor and a gaze that cut through fabric and flesh. While the rest of the men postured, Alessio Moretti stood still. Regal. Ruined. Beautiful in a brutal way.

And he was walking toward her.

Someone said her name. She didn't care who.

Her heart beat like a war drum against her ribs.

"Miss Romano," Alessio said as he reached her, offering a gloved hand. "May I have this dance?"

It wasn't a question. It was an invitation to a battle she wasn't ready to decline.

She took his hand.

The contact sent heat up her arm, into her throat. His palm was rough, calloused beneath the silk. Like a man who had built things—and broken more.

The waltz began.

They moved like enemies pretending to be lovers.

A spin. A step. A shared breath too close.

"You clean up well," she said sweetly, letting her venom drip like honey. "I expected blood on your cuffs."

He smiled—just enough to scare her.

"I keep it off my suit. Never off my hands."

Their feet moved in perfect sync. Their eyes did not.

"You've made quite the impression tonight," she said. "Even my father looks impressed. Not easy to do."

"Your father's impressed by dogs that don't bite when ordered."

"And you?"

"I bite when I *want* to."

Her heart skipped.

Their bodies swayed closer, the music curling around them like smoke.

"Tell me, Moretti," she said softly, "what's your real game here?"

"To win."

"And what do you want?"

His grip on her waist tightened—just slightly, just enough.

"You."

The word wasn't flirtation.

It was war.

Something Shifts

The music changed, but neither of them moved.

Her hand still rested on his shoulder, his palm still pressed against the curve of her waist. One step forward, one step back—they danced, but neither of them remembered the rhythm.

The ballroom faded into a blur of silk and shadows. The crowd disappeared into silence.

It was just him. Just her.

And the dangerous space between their mouths.

It should've been another performance. Another dance for diplomacy. Another staged display for their fathers' political theater. But something had cracked open beneath the surface, raw and uninvited.

Isabella felt it first.

A shift in his touch—firm, possessive, yet reverent. His thumb brushed along her lower back, not in dominance, but in quiet warning. Not to her. To himself.

Then it was in his gaze.

His eyes, which had always been sharp and calculating, now burned with something far more human. Desire. Conflict. Memory.

He was staring at her like he'd been cursed to.

And worse—she didn't look away.

She tilted her head slightly, heart pounding as if her own blood had betrayed her, and let herself *see* him.

Not the enemy.

Not the threat.

Not the Moretti heir.

But the boy beneath the rage. The storm buried under suits and scars. The survivor who hadn't just inherited violence—he had *been forged in it.*

And for one long, terrible moment, she felt seen.

Not as a daughter. Not as a bride-to-be. Not as a weapon or a name.

As a woman.

And God help her—she liked it.

Their bodies pressed too close. Her breath was his. Her pulse a secret against his wrist.

She should've stepped away.

He should've let go.

But neither did.

Because the battlefield had changed. The lines blurred. Enemies didn't breathe each other in.

But they just had.

She hated him. She wanted him.

And that was the most dangerous truth of all.

The music ended, but the moment lingered like perfume and poison.

She turned first, retreating into the crowd before the weight of her emotions made her betray them. Her spine stayed straight, her chin lifted with practiced poise, but her pulse throbbed with something she didn't have a name for.

He watched her walk away—every sway of her hips, every flick of defiance in her step. And he knew.

She was a problem he hadn't anticipated.

A distraction he couldn't afford.

A temptation wrapped in enemy silk.

But she was more than that.

She was fire.

And fire, no matter how beautiful, was meant to consume.

As she reached the far end of the ballroom, she paused—just once, barely a breath—before disappearing down the corridor of her father's empire.

And then, from behind her, his voice cut through the air.

Low.

Lethal.

Intimate.

"Then scream," he said, voice like smoke and steel.

And he turned away—
like he already owned her soul
…or planned to.

CHAPTER 4

- Broken Vows -

HIS ENEMIES CALLED him a ghost. But in the shadows, Alessio was very much alive—and watching.

The ballroom's afterglow still lingered in the walls of the Romano estate, like perfume clinging to skin. But Alessio had already slipped into the quiet corridors, where velvet and violence coexisted without question.

He moved like a shadow beneath chandeliers and security cameras, stepping into the side parlor where Luca awaited—his consigliere and closest confidant, the only man in this world who didn't flinch at his silence.

Luca was nursing a bourbon, suit rumpled from hours of diplomacy. He raised a brow when Alessio entered, but didn't speak until the door clicked shut behind them.

"Bellini's a snake," Luca said simply, handing over a folder. "Thought you'd want to see this."

Alessio took it, flipping it open with a precision that had nothing to do with impatience and everything to do with discipline. Inside—photos, transcripts, surveillance logs. Bellini's movements over the past month.

"You were right," Luca added. "He's not loyal to either family. He's playing both."

Alessio's jaw tightened.

In the photos, Marco Bellini smiled too easily. He met with men who owed no allegiance to Moretti or Romano. He lingered in nightclubs owned by foreign cartels, whispered into phones with no traceable line, and most recently—handed an envelope to a known arms broker in Marseille.

Sloppy. Dangerous. Opportunistic.

"He's not just ambitious," Alessio murmured. "He's reckless."

"And your princess is supposed to marry him in four weeks."

He hated how that made something inside him shift.

Isabella wasn't his. Wasn't meant to be. But the image of her dancing in that black dress, all thorns and fire, clung to his brain like smoke. The way she'd looked at Bellini across the ballroom—stiff, guarded. Like a woman waiting for a sentence.

"She won't," Alessio said quietly.

Luca leaned forward. "Is that strategy talking? Or something else?"

Alessio didn't answer.

But he didn't need to.

He closed the folder, cold resolve settling behind his ribs like iron.

Bellini wasn't a threat. He was a target. And Alessio always eliminated his targets.

The Garden Incident

Night had unfurled across the estate like a velvet noose.

Alessio moved through it like it belonged to him.

He'd memorized the layout the moment he arrived: two wings, three security blind spots, four potential exits. But it was the garden he lingered near now—because he saw her slip through the stone archway beneath the rose-covered trellis.

Isabella.

Alone. Bare-shouldered. Breathless.

The moonlight kissed her hair like silver fire, and for a moment, he hated the instinct that pulled him toward her. Hated the weakness of wanting to see her when he should be watching everyone else.

But then she wasn't alone.

Marco appeared behind her.

Alessio stilled in the shadows.

At first, the conversation was low. Heated whispers. Gestures sharp enough to slice.

Then it shifted.

Marco stepped forward, crowding her space.

Isabella pushed him back—small hands against his chest, spine straight with pride. But Marco's smile twisted, and his hand shot out, grabbing her wrist.

Hard.

Too hard.

Alessio saw the moment her expression shifted from fury to pain.

And that was enough.

He was across the garden before the thought finished forming, silent as vengeance, dark as war.

Marco didn't hear him coming.

Not until a hand clamped around his shoulder and yanked him back with force that slammed him against the trellis.

"What the—"

Alessio pressed him into the stone with one forearm across his throat.

"Touch her again," he said, voice low, lethal, "and I'll break every bone in your hand."

Marco choked on his shock. "What the hell are you—"

"I said," Alessio leaned in, breath ice-cold against his cheek, "touch her again and I'll cut your fingers off and feed them to your fucking dog."

Marco shoved back, red with rage. "You think you can come here and make threats? This is *Romano* ground!"

"And I'm not afraid to stain it."

The tension rippled outward like a shot.

Isabella stood behind them, stunned. Her wrist red where Marco had grabbed her. Her lips parted in something between shock and fury and confusion.

Marco looked at her, then at Alessio. "He's just mad he can't have you."

Alessio didn't move. Didn't blink.

He just smiled.

"Don't mistake my silence for restraint," he said. "I came here for peace. But if you give me a reason to start a war, I won't hesitate."

Intervention

The garden had returned to stillness, but the air was heavy —coiled with words unspoken, with something dangerous blooming between them.

Alessio stood in the dim lamplight, his breath calm but his heart anything but.

Across from him, Isabella Romano looked like she belonged to another world—moonlight caught in her hair, shadows softening the sharpness of her features. But the red mark blooming on her wrist didn't lie.

He watched her as she rubbed it absently, her expression carefully composed, the silence stretching between them like a taut wire.

"You shouldn't have done that," she said at last. Her voice was quiet, but there was no softness in it—only pride, tightly leashed.

"You had no right."

"I had every right," Alessio said simply.

"To what? Step in like some knight in a suit?" Her laugh was bitter, humorless.

"This isn't a fairytale, Moretti. There are no heroes here."

"No," he agreed. "Only villains."

She stopped rubbing her wrist, her chin lifting with defiance. "Then don't pretend to be something you're not."

"I'm not pretending." He took a step forward, and though she didn't move, he felt the way her body tensed—ready to flee or fight.

"I'm telling you the truth. Marco is a coward. And cowards are dangerous when they're desperate."

"I can handle him."

"I don't doubt that. But tonight he didn't care that you said no. Tonight, you were nothing more than a pawn to him."

"And what am I to you?"

The question landed like a blade.

Alessio didn't answer right away. He looked at her—the way her eyes burned beneath the bravado, the way she masked fear with fire. Her strength wasn't something she wore.

It was embedded in her bones, forged in silence, in expectations too heavy for anyone so young.

He saw her.

Not just the daughter of a rival. Not just a bargaining chip in a bloody game.

He saw the woman behind the name.

"I don't know yet," he said finally. "But I know you're not a pawn."

"Don't romanticize it," she snapped. "We're weapons on opposite sides of a war."

"Maybe," he said, stepping closer again. "But I don't want to see yours turned against you."

That silenced her.

For a long, suspended moment, she just stared at him—like she was trying to figure out what kind of game he was playing. But Alessio wasn't playing. Not tonight. He had come into the Romano estate with blood in his mouth and strategy in his veins. He hadn't planned on interference. And he sure as hell hadn't planned on *her*.

He reached into his inner pocket, pulled out a sleek metal case, and opened it—not to reveal a weapon, but a small tin of salve.

"What is that?" she asked warily.

"For your wrist," he said, handing it to her. "It's something my mother made. For bruises."

She hesitated. "That's sweet. Should I be touched or terrified?"

"You should be smart and use it before it turns purple."

She accepted the tin slowly, their fingers brushing just briefly—and it sent something white-hot jolting through both of them.

She looked down. "Why are you really here, Alessio?"

His name in her voice did something to him.

"I came for the peace treaty," he said. "But I stayed for the truth."

Her gaze flicked up. "And what truth is that?"

"That the Romanos may rule this city, but their kingdom is rotting from the inside."

"And you think you're here to save it?"

"No," he said, with a bitter smile. "I'm here to burn it down."

She inhaled sharply. "Including me?"

His voice turned soft. "Not you."

The silence between them now wasn't sharp—it was thick, velvet, intimate.

"Be careful, Isabella," he said again. "You don't need to be afraid of men like Marco. You need to be afraid of the ones who smile when they hurt you."

She looked up at him, eyes wide, expression caught somewhere between disbelief and something far more dangerous.

"And which one are you?" she whispered.

Alessio stepped back, just enough to let the distance grow—but not enough to break the moment.

"I'm the one who doesn't lie to you."

And for the first time, she didn't have an answer.

They stood in silence as the wind stirred the roses, as the stone walls of the estate listened in on a secret neither of them dared name.

Isabella gripped the tin of salve, fingers trembling only slightly. Alessio's eyes lingered on the bruises that would bloom like violets on her skin by morning—and on the steel in her spine that refused to let her falter.

She didn't thank him.

And he didn't expect her to.

He started to walk away.

But at the edge of the garden, just beneath the arch where the moonlight filtered through leaves like cathedral glass, he paused.

His voice, when it came, was quiet—but it held the weight of a war not yet fought.

"Next time he touches you," Alessio said without turning back,
"He won't walk away."

Then he disappeared into the darkness, leaving her with nothing but the scent of roses, the echo of threat disguised as protection, and the ghost of a man who had come to destroy her world—and might just take her heart instead.

CHAPTER 5

- The Kiss -

SHE FOUND HIM in the east corridor—where the shadows clung to stone walls and whispered of things better left buried.

The world outside the estate still slept, but Isabella's blood boiled with a heat that would not be silenced.

Alessio Moretti stood by the window, the glow of a cigarette ember painting his cheekbones in firelight. He looked carved from war, every line of him too sharp to belong in this house of porcelain lies.

"Why did you do it?" Her voice cracked the silence like glass.

He didn't turn. He didn't need to. She felt the weight of his attention settle over her anyway.

"You're going to have to be more specific."

"You know what I mean." She walked closer, each step measured, each breath shallow. "Last night. In the garden. Marco."

He finally looked at her.

His gaze was unreadable—ancient and violent in its restraint. "You looked like you needed saving."

"I don't need saving." Her voice snapped like a whip. "I need answers."

"I didn't do it for you." A lie. Too clean to be true.

"Then who?" she demanded.

A pause. His eyes darkened, stormy with something she couldn't name. "Maybe I did it for myself."

"Because you hate Marco?" she pressed.

"No." He tossed the cigarette out the window, its spark dying in the cold. "Because I hate watching someone who still has fight left in her get crushed."

That silenced her.

Because it wasn't the answer she expected—and yet it burned in her chest like truth.

"I didn't ask for your pity."

"Good," he said, taking a step forward, "because that wasn't what I gave."

He was too close now.

Close enough that she could smell the faint scent of tobacco and spice and something darker—like leather soaked in memory.

"You think you know me," she whispered.

"I don't," he replied. "But I see you."

And something inside her broke.

There were no words after that.

Only breath.

Only the impossible distance between two people born to be enemies, standing in a silence so thick it hummed with fury and fire.

He looked at her like he was memorizing a blueprint he had no right to build.

She looked at him like he was already her ruin.

And then—it happened.

No fanfare. No warning.

One second she was glaring, and the next—

His lips were on hers.

It wasn't soft.

It wasn't gentle.

It was a crash—violent and raw, the kind of kiss you give someone when you're too furious to speak and too desperate to walk away.

Her hands were in his hair before she could think. His were at her waist, pulling her to him like he had every right. The heat was unbearable. His mouth devoured hers like she was oxygen and he'd been suffocating for years.

It was clumsy in its hunger, perfect in its imperfection.

Her back hit the wall with a thud, but she didn't flinch. His teeth grazed her bottom lip, and she gasped—and that sound undid him.

He deepened the kiss.

Their hatred melted between them, twisted into something unholy—lust weaponized.

She didn't want to stop.

God help her, she wanted more.

But when his hand slid up her ribs, a thread of clarity ripped through the fog.

She tore herself away like she'd touched fire.

Aftermath

Silence crashed around them, louder than any argument

could've been.

Isabella's chest rose and fell in sharp, uneven pulls, as though she'd just run a marathon—but the only thing she'd run from was herself.

She didn't move at first. Couldn't. Her body was frozen in the ghost of his touch, still reeling from the raw heat of his mouth on hers. The imprint of his hands burned through the fabric of her dress, as if he'd marked her in ways no one else could see.

Her eyes flicked up to meet his.

Alessio wasn't composed either. He stood a few feet away, chest heaving, lips parted slightly, the faintest tremor in his jaw betraying just how much control he'd lost.

And for a man like him, *losing control* was an act of war.

It terrified her.

Not because he was dangerous—but because he wasn't supposed to look like he *regretted it*. He was supposed to be smug. Cruel. Detached.

Instead, he looked almost... wrecked.

He ran a hand through his hair, and for a moment, the ice around him cracked. "That shouldn't have happened."

"No," she whispered. "It shouldn't have."

But neither of them moved.

Seconds stretched like glass, waiting to shatter.

Isabella stepped back. One step. Then another. Putting distance where there had been none.

It wasn't enough.

"I don't do this," she said, voice hollow. "I don't... kiss people I hate."

Alessio's laugh was low, bitter. "You don't hate me. Not

completely."

Her spine straightened like a blade. "Don't presume to know what I feel."

His eyes darkened, colder now. "Too late for that."

He turned, as if walking away would undo what had just happened.

But she wasn't ready to let him go—not yet.

"You're the enemy," she said, each word stabbing at her chest like a shard of guilt.

Alessio paused, his back to her. "So are you."

He didn't look back when he disappeared down the corridor.

And that made it worse.

Because it meant the moment meant something.

Not just to her.

But to him too.

She leaned against the cold marble wall, a hand pressed to her mouth like it could erase the truth.

Only it couldn't.

She could still taste him.

And that taste was going to haunt her every damn night.

Her lips still burned.
And her heart—foolish, reckless traitor that it was—no longer beat only for herself.

It had whispered his name.

And in that kiss, in that brief, stolen breath between war and surrender... Isabella Romano realized the most unforgivable truth of all:

She hadn't kissed her enemy.

She'd kissed the only man who'd ever seen her.

And that was a betrayal far more dangerous than anything her family could ever inflict.

Because this time, the wound was hers to carry.

And it was bleeding from the inside out.

CHAPTER 6

- When the Lion Bows -

THERE ARE TWO KINDS of men in this world: those who kneel for love, and those who kill it first.

Alessio Moretti was raised to be the latter.

He walked alone through the private cemetery nestled deep behind the Moretti estate, where only the ghosts of his bloodline could hear the confessions he refused to speak aloud.

The winter fog clung to the gravestones like mourning shrouds, and under his leather shoes, the earth still felt unsettled—like it remembered the blood it had swallowed.

He stopped in front of his father's headstone.

Lorenzo Moretti
Il Leone. Il Padre. Il Re.
1964 – 2008

He didn't speak for a long time. Just stood, the wind slicing through his coat like the steel of old memories.

Then finally—*"I kissed her."*

It came out hoarse. Ugly. Confessional.

He crouched slowly, brushing a leaf from the stone. "She's Romano. The enemy. I should hate her. I *do* hate her. But—" he exhaled, his voice breaking into a low, bitter laugh "—she tastes like rebellion. Like ruin."

His hands trembled. Not from cold. From the kind of rage that only ever came when power met power—and neither bent.

Alessio looked at the soil, as if the answers were buried deeper than the bones beneath. "You told me love was weakness. But *what if this isn't love*? What if it's something worse?"

A pause. The kind that wrapped silence around the throat.

"I think I want to *own* her, Papa. To break her down and build her again. As mine. Not theirs. Never theirs."

He didn't ask for forgiveness.

He knew the dead didn't forgive. They only waited to be avenged.

A Warning

His uncle was waiting.

Salvatore Moretti stood beside a sleek, obsidian town car parked under the canopy of barren trees at the edge of the Moretti family cemetery. The storm had not yet broken, but the clouds hung low and heavy with unspoken threats.

A cigarette burned between his fingers, its smoke curling like a ghost's breath in the frigid air.

He didn't look at Alessio right away.

Instead, he exhaled smoke slowly, deliberately, eyes fixed on the gravestones that stretched like silent witnesses to sins unburied.

"Graves make men sentimental," Salvatore murmured. "That's dangerous."

Alessio didn't answer. The silence between them was thick—decades of unspoken truths and blood-soaked loyalty embedded in every breath.

Salvatore turned at last, his expression unreadable but his

gaze cutting. "Tell me it's not the Romano girl."

Alessio's jaw clenched. A muscle ticked in his cheek.

"That's what I thought," his uncle said. "You think I don't see it? I've seen the way you watch her. Like she's the last truth in a world made of lies. Like she's your salvation. She isn't."

"She's not her father," Alessio said, his voice low, as if even saying it felt like a confession too loud.

Salvatore snorted. "You think that matters? You think blood isn't fate? Don Emilio bred her for this life. Just like we bred you. The only difference is—she knows how to wear the crown without it breaking her neck."

Alessio's eyes narrowed. "She's not like him."

"No. She's smarter," Salvatore shot back. "Don't let that silk and fire fool you. She's a weapon. Beautiful, yes. But dangerous. And you... you're already bleeding."

He took another drag of his cigarette, then flicked the ash to the ground, watching it disappear into the frostbitten soil.

"You want her? Fine," he said. "Want her body. Hell, take it if it'll burn this sickness out of you. But keep your heart locked behind your ribs, Alessio. Tight. Triple-barred. You can't afford soft—not now. Not ever."

"I don't have a heart," Alessio replied flatly, eyes hard.

"Good." Salvatore dropped the cigarette and crushed it under his boot. "Then don't grow one."

He started toward the car, but paused with his hand on the door. "Love is for men who don't lead empires. Love is for poets and fools."

Then, with a final glance over his shoulder, he said it quieter— almost like he regretted how well he knew it.

"And we don't get to be either."

The car door slammed shut. The engine purred like a predator in the dark.

But Alessio didn't move.

He stood there long after the car disappeared into the road curling away from the dead.

Because it was already too late.

He had kissed her.

And in that kiss, something had cracked.

Not just the walls he'd spent a lifetime building, but the foundations beneath them.

Cracks had a way of turning into ruins.

And Alessio Moretti knew—he was already halfway to collapse.

The Decision

That night, the storm finally broke.

Lightning spiderwebbed the sky in jagged veins of light. Thunder rolled like gunfire. The wind howled through the Moretti estate, shaking the shutters, rattling the windows. But inside his bedroom, Alessio stood silent and still—untouched by the violence outside.

The world could rage all it wanted.

The war was already inside him.

He stood on his balcony, rain slashing sideways, his tailored suit soaked through. He didn't feel the cold. He didn't care.

He only saw her.

Isabella.

Daughter of the man who'd taken everything from him.

Daughter of the empire he was raised to crush.

She should have been a pawn.

She should have been a stepping stone.

Instead, she'd become a goddamn earthquake.

He could still taste her on his lips. Could still feel the way her breath had hitched just before he kissed her, like even her rebellion wanted to surrender to him. That kiss hadn't been sweet.

It had been war. A declaration. A promise neither of them knew how to keep.

And it undid him.

Because it wasn't just about the heat anymore. It wasn't just about the way her body arched with anger or how her voice turned to steel when she was afraid.

It was about the look in her eyes when she let him see past the walls.

The moment her armor cracked, and he saw the girl buried beneath the fury.

He wasn't supposed to want her.

But now, Alessio couldn't breathe without her name in his chest.

She was the enemy.

And he'd never wanted anything more.

He turned back inside, rain still dripping from his dark hair, his shirt plastered to his skin. He pulled off the jacket, tossed it aside. His boots echoed as he crossed the marble floor to the mirror.

And what stared back at him wasn't a prince.

It wasn't a king.

It was a boy with blood on his hands and war in his veins.

A boy who'd never been taught what to do with want.

A boy who'd been told love was weakness, and vengeance was virtue.

He touched the medallion around his neck. His father's. Still warm from his skin.

Don Lorenzo Moretti would have never approved. Would have raged. Would have reminded him that the only way to survive in this world was to take everything before someone took it from you.

But Alessio wasn't sure he believed that anymore.

Not when he looked at her.

Not when he remembered the way she looked back.

He whispered it like a secret. Like a sin. "I won't let her burn alone."

Because he knew what came next.

He couldn't walk away from this. Couldn't put her in a box and pretend she was just another tactic.

This wasn't strategy.

This wasn't control.

It was hunger. It was heat. It was a dangerous, roaring thing that refused to be silenced.

She wasn't his weakness.

She was his edge.

And if the world demanded he choose between the kingdom and the girl?

He'd choose her.

He'd burn down every throne.

If she was fire, he'd let her burn him.

But he'd burn her right back.

Because this wasn't love.
It was obsession.
It was war dressed as longing.
It was the quiet beginning of an inferno that would consume them both.

And Alessio Moretti had never feared the fire.
Only the silence it left behind.

But now, silence had a name.

Isabella.

CHAPTER 7

- The Night -

A KISS IS NEVER just a kiss when given by the enemy—and received like salvation.

That's what haunted her, not his lips.
Not the searing heat of it.
But the truth it had dragged out of her, mercilessly and without permission.

Isabella sat before her mirror, fingers trembling against the ivory handle of her hairbrush, but her eyes didn't see her reflection.

She stared through it, beyond it, to that moment in the corridor where breath had become a currency she could no longer afford.

Alessio Moretti had taken something she hadn't meant to give. And worse—he hadn't asked.

And yet…
She'd given it anyway.

Her mouth still tasted like him—ash and fury. Her skin still remembered the pressure of his hands, not in domination, but desperation. Like touching her had been necessary for survival.

It wasn't the kiss itself that had her reeling.
It was what it revealed.

She wasn't immune. She wasn't untouched. She wasn't safe.

From him. From herself.

She dropped the brush. It clattered against the marble floor like a shot fired in silence.

Outside her window, the sky hung heavy with stars and secrets. Her pulse fluttered like a trapped bird behind her ribs.

How do you walk back from that?
How do you return to chains once you've tasted heat?

A Visit from Her Past

The knock on her bedroom door came just after midnight.

Soft. Measured. Dangerous in its calm.

Isabella turned, spine straightening like a violin string pulled too tight. Only one person ever knocked like that anymore.

She opened the door and found Luca—older now, the boy who once snuck her lemon candies during Mass, now a man in a suit too sharp for friendship and eyes too tired for innocence.

"Luca," she breathed. "You shouldn't be here."

"I never should've left," he replied, stepping in without permission. "But I came with a warning. One you won't like."

Her heart dipped.

"Is it my father?"

Luca's jaw tightened. "It's *him.* The Moretti heir. Alessio."

Her breath caught—just a flicker.

"He looks at you like a man who plans to ruin you," he said flatly. "And men like that? They don't fail."

"You don't know him," she replied, too quickly.

And that, she realized, was the first betrayal. Because she didn't know him either.

Not really.

But something inside her had started to believe she could. That the boy behind the steel-blue gaze—the one who burned with purpose and poison—was more than a weapon.

Luca stepped closer, lowering his voice. "Whatever game you think you're playing, Isa… you won't win."

"I'm not playing."

He studied her a beat longer, eyes sad. "Then you'll lose even faster."

She didn't respond.
Because losing—if it meant him—was starting to sound a lot like freedom.

The Piano Room

The house was asleep, or at least pretending to be.

Isabella wandered the halls like a wraith, silk nightdress clinging to her like shadows. Her feet found their way to the only room that ever made sense—the piano room, hidden behind carved oak doors and silence.

She sat before the grand Steinway like she always did when sleep refused her.

Her fingers found the keys and pressed them gently, like an apology. The notes were low and mournful, a song of want and warning. She didn't remember what it was called. Only that her mother used to hum it when storms threatened.

Halfway through the melody, she felt it.

That pull.

The sense of being watched—no, *witnessed.*

She didn't stop playing.

"You play like you're trying to forget something," came a voice from the dark corner of the room.

Her fingers froze. Not because she was afraid.

But because she already knew who it was.

Alessio stepped forward from the shadows. No suit tonight. No tie. Just black and bare forearms and a face carved from vengeance and velvet.

"How long have you been there?" she asked.

"Long enough."

The silence thickened. Her hands dropped from the keys.

"You shouldn't be here."

"I never should've come back to this city," he replied, eyes gleaming. "But here we are."

She turned toward him, arms crossing her chest. "What do you want, Moretti?"

"You."

The word dropped between them like a detonated secret. Quiet. Final.

Her throat tightened. "Why?"

He walked toward her slowly, deliberately, as though she were a question he intended to unravel one thread at a time.

"Because you don't flinch when I get close," he said, stopping inches from her. "Because when you lie, your eyes betray you. Because you taste like a dare."

"You're not allowed to say things like that to me."

He reached out, trailing a finger along her jaw, not touching—hovering.

"I'm not allowed to do a lot of things," he murmured.

The air crackled.

"Why are you really here?" she whispered.

His hand dropped.

"I don't know anymore," he said honestly. "Once, it was to destroy your family. Now…"

"Now?"

He stepped back.

"Now, I come here just to see if you'll still look at me the same way."

She should've left. Should've run.

Instead, she asked, "And if I don't?"

His smile was a tragedy written in skin. "Then maybe I'll finally stop looking back."

Isabella watched him slip away like a shadow returning to the night.

She didn't follow.

She sat back down, touched the keys, and this time when she played, the song sounded like fire licking at lace.

She didn't sleep that night.

Not because of fear.

But because his words played louder in her mind than any lullaby ever could.

"Do you dream of burning, Isabella?"

"Because I do."

And for the first time, she wondered:

What if the fire didn't destroy her?

What if it made her more than they ever allowed her to be?

CHAPTER 8

- The Red Ledger -

EVERY MAN HAS A ledger. Some ink it in blood. Alessio carved his into the bones of memory.

The Moretti estate was still cloaked in shadows when Alessio summoned his most trusted inner circle. Matteo, his consigliere, took the seat to his right, as always. Beside him sat Nico, the enforcer whose silence spoke in bruises and broken bones.

Across the table, Sofia—the only woman ever allowed in this sanctum—held a glass of bourbon and a gaze like tempered steel. They were family, not by blood, but by the brutal choices that made blood irrelevant.

On the table sat photos. Dock shipments. Cargo manifests. Surveillance images. And one familiar face.

Marco Bellini.

Alessio tapped the grainy photo with the end of his pen. "This was taken at Dock Nine. Three nights ago."

Nico leaned in. "That's a Romano-controlled port."

"Was," Alessio corrected coldly. "It's now a smuggling tunnel with Bellini's fingerprints all over it."

Matteo raised a brow. "You sure?"

Alessio slid another photo forward. Marco, talking to a

man with a scar under his eye—a known associate of Emilio Romano's weapons supplier.

Matteo whistled low. "That's a fucking betrayal."

"No," Alessio said, calm as glass. "That's a declaration of war."

Sofia's eyes narrowed. "Does Isabella know?"

He didn't answer.

Did it matter?

She had kissed him like he was salvation—but she was still her father's daughter.

And Marco Bellini, that snake in silk, was still her intended.

For now.

The Interrogation

The rain fell like bullets on the pavement outside the old slaughterhouse at the edge of the city—the place where ghosts liked to whisper and sins could be buried in concrete.

Inside, Alessio waited in the dark.

Marco Bellini was late. Or maybe just too stupid to realize that being summoned here wasn't a suggestion.

The steel door groaned open.

Two of Alessio's men dragged Marco in, his custom-tailored suit rumpled, a thin line of blood trailing from the corner of his mouth. He looked less like a fiancé and more like a rat that had scurried too close to the fire.

Alessio didn't speak right away. He stood with his back to the room, watching the rain trace crooked veins down the windowpane.

His silence was a scalpel—it carved nerves more deeply than threats ever could.

"Alessio," Marco rasped, trying to stand straight. "This isn't necessary—"

"You're late," Alessio said, his voice low and controlled, like a knife unsheathed in a cathedral. "I don't tolerate disrespect. Not from enemies. And certainly not from traitors."

"I'm not—"

"Careful." He turned, and Marco flinched. "Lies taste worse when I already know the truth."

He stepped forward, every movement deliberate. Calculated. Predatory. There was nothing theatrical in Alessio's fury—it was the kind that simmered low, like embers waiting for skin.

"We traced the dock shipments to a warehouse you lease under a fake name," Alessio said. "You've been rerouting my supply lines. You thought you were clever."

"I was trying to survive!" Marco blurted. "Don Emilio—he threatened my family."

Alessio's smile was ice. "And so you chose to crawl into his bed while courting his daughter? Or is Isabella just another pawn in your game?"

Marco's eyes darted, guilt flickering like a match. "I didn't mean to hurt her."

"No," Alessio said, stepping close enough for Marco to feel the heat radiating off him, "but you did."

The room stilled. Even the rain seemed to hesitate.

Alessio's hand twitched toward the blade sheathed under his coat, but he stopped himself. Not yet. Not here. Isabella would ask questions. And she was already asking too many.

"I should end you," he said, voice low. "But she'd notice. And I'm not ready for her to see that part of me."

He leaned in, his mouth brushing Marco's ear.

"But I want you to wake up every morning wondering if today

is the day your lungs fill with blood."

Then he stepped back, as if the conversation were over. As if Marco were already dead.

"Let him go," Alessio ordered.

One of his men hesitated. "You sure?"

Alessio's stare turned lethal. "Yes."

As they dragged Marco out, limp and shaken, Alessio lit a cigarette with the same hand that had once held a gun to his own temple as a teenager. He'd made it through that darkness. He wasn't sure Marco would.

Because vengeance wasn't just about death.

Sometimes, the slow rot of fear was far more satisfying.

THE LEDGER

Later that night, Alessio returned to the one place no one dared enter—his father's study.

The air still smelled like him. Cigars and saffron and something deeper—like power that refused to decay.

He lit the old lamp on the mahogany desk and pulled out the red leather-bound book that had been locked away behind the false panel.

His father's ledger.

The last testament of a king who had built an empire in silence and fire.

Alessio opened it with reverence, the cracked spine groaning like it remembered the weight of blood.

Page after page, he traced names.

Allies. Enemies. Debts paid and unpaid. Secrets never spoken aloud. It was a map of shadows. Every red mark was a warning. Every circle, a target.

And then he saw it.

Emilio Romano.

Circled. Not once. But three times.

The ink had bled through the page like it had been carved in rage.

Beneath the name was one line in his father's handwriting—sharp, angular, and final.

"He broke the pact. He stole the fire. He must burn."

Alessio's breath caught.

His father had known.

He had suspected Don Emilio long before the explosion. The whispers, the betrayals, the slow erosion of loyalty—it had all been here, buried beneath pages of polite silence.

His fingers trembled as he turned the next page, and the next, and the next.

Photographs.

Of the Romano estate. Of Marco with unfamiliar men. Of documents that had passed hands behind closed doors.

Proof. Not just of betrayal.

Of conspiracy.

And then… her name.

Isabella.

Not circled. Not crossed out. Just written… once.

Isabella Romano.

A single ink drop beneath her name. Not a dot. Not an error.

A tear stain.

Alessio closed the book slowly, spine clicking shut like the lid of a coffin.

This wasn't about empires anymore.

This was about his father.

About the boy who had held his corpse in smoke and fire.

And about the girl with the name of a traitor and the eyes of a storm he couldn't outrun.

He stood in the dark for a long time, medallion clutched in one hand, the ledger in the other.

And when he finally spoke, it wasn't to anyone in the room.

"I'll bury them all," he whispered to the ghost that still lingered. "But not her. Never her."

CHAPTER 9

- Silk and Steel -

THERE WAS A SILENCE in the Romano estate that morning—not the kind of silence born of peace, but the kind that followed a funeral no one had the courage to hold.

The maids flitted like ghosts around Isabella, measuring, adjusting, pinning satin against her ribs as if she were some offering to be laid at the altar of family allegiance. The room smelled of roses, steamed fabric, and barely concealed nerves.

Her mother hovered near the mirror, sipping champagne far too early, eyes glassy as she murmured about elegance and purity, about how white would make her look like a dove.

Isabella chose red.

A gown the shade of blood. Fitted to the waist, silk that clung like sin, with a neckline that dared to show she was more than a pawn.

More than a daughter. More than the bride-to-be of a man she did not love.

"No," she said, voice calm and clear, when the seamstress hesitated. "This one."

Her mother's protest was immediate. "Red is vulgar, Isabella. It's a color for widows and whores."

"Then it suits me perfectly," she replied, her tone edged like glass.

They stared at each other across a chasm of generations and choices neither of them had made willingly. But Isabella did not yield.

Because this night would not be her submission.

It would be her warning.

Her declaration.

Let them see the fire before it burns the whole house down.

A Dangerous Gift

The package came while the sky turned bronze outside her windows, the dusk bleeding into the room like a secret no one wanted spoken.

A black box.

Unmarked.

Inside—an antique dagger with a serpent-wrapped hilt and a blade older than her bloodline.

And a note.

Just three words, written in his hand:

For your protection.

She stared at it, fingers trembling not with fear, but recognition. The hilt bore the Moretti crest on its spine, but it wasn't his. No—this dagger once belonged to her grandmother. She had seen it in old photos, clutched in the folds of a wedding gown before the Romanos buried it under years of theft and lies.

How had he found it?

Why had he given it back?

Her pulse fluttered like wings caught in a cage, her thoughts stuttering between fury and fascination. Alessio Moretti, heir of blood and vendetta, was gifting her a piece of herself she didn't even know she'd lost.

A weapon.

A memory.

A message.

He was telling her something no one else dared: that she was not safe in her own home.

That he knew it.

And he would not let her face the wolves unarmed.

The blade was cool in her palm. A contradiction. Like the man who had sent it.

Outside her door, her mother was already shouting orders about the car. The gala was minutes away.

Isabella opened her wardrobe and peeled back the folds of her crimson dress.

There. Beneath the layers of silk and bone, she fastened the dagger against her thigh, the leather strap biting into skin.

She wasn't sure if it was the blade or her heartbeat that throbbed against her flesh.

Maybe it didn't matter.

Because tonight, she would wear both like armor.

The Mirror Moment

The room had grown too quiet, as if the walls themselves were holding their breath.

Isabella stood in front of the gilded mirror, her blood-red gown spilling like a wound across the marble floor.

The seamstress had left, whispering pleasantries that didn't touch her ears. The door clicked shut. Silence pressed in.

And there she was.

Not Isabella Romano, daughter of Don Emilio. Not the prize bride being dressed like bait for a man she would never love. But something else. Something sharpened. Something cracking open.

Her fingers trembled slightly as she lifted the velvet box Alessio had sent her.

Inside, the dagger gleamed with age and violence. Ivory-handled. Inlaid with roses and thorns. The blade still smelled faintly of steel and smoke—like a memory. Like blood long dried but never forgotten.

Her breath caught.

This belonged to her grandmother. She remembered it, dimly—stories whispered by her mother when she was still alive. The blade had been stolen during the Romano family's rise to power.

Claimed by her father's men as spoils of a "negotiation" gone wrong. She hadn't seen it in years.

How Alessio had found it, she didn't know. But he had.

And he'd returned it with a note written in the same ink as danger:
"For protection. Use it."

It wasn't a gift. It was a mirror. A reflection of the war she was becoming.

She lifted the dagger to her face and stared at her reflection in the blade—distorted, fractured, truer than the glass could ever show.

The silk gown, the pinned hair, the ruby earrings—none of it disguised the ache growing in her bones.

What they didn't see—what they would never see—was the rage carved beneath her ribs.

The scream sitting silent on her tongue. The daughter who had learned to smile like her mother but cut like her father.

She pressed the dagger's flat edge to her collarbone. It was cold. Honest.

Then slowly, reverently, she lifted her gown and slid the blade into a hidden garter stitched into the lace. The dagger hugged her thigh like a secret. Like a promise.

In the mirror, her eyes looked different now.

Not softer. Not harder.

Just awake.

That night, she didn't cry.

She didn't shatter.

She became steel wrapped in velvet.

As the music of the gala rose from the floors below, Isabella stood alone in her room—her hand resting just above her thigh, where the dagger waited like a pulse.

She wasn't going down those stairs to play her part. She was going down to begin something else entirely.

She would walk into the lion's den.

She would wear red like war.

And with every smile she gave, with every lie she told, she'd be carving her escape into the walls of the house that caged her.

Because now, she carried more than lace and obligation.

She carried a weapon.

A choice.

And the memory of a boy with haunted eyes who had returned a piece of her past—and maybe something of her future too.

The dagger was cold against her thigh.

But in her chest, something was beginning to burn.

And Isabella Romano had never been so ready to set fire to everything that claimed to own her.

CHAPTER 10

- The Gala of Lies -

THE VILLA SHIMMERED under chandeliers and chandeliers of lies. Alessio Moretti stepped out of the shadow of a black sedan, mask in place—bone-white and blank.

His tailored suit clung to him like sin, the fabric whispering with every calculated step. The Moretti crest was absent. No insignia. No announcement.

And yet, the silence bowed for him.

He entered the ballroom not as a guest, but as a god of war slipping past velvet-curtained pleasantries. The music swelled—violins, polite laughter, heels against marble—and he moved through it like a ghost no one dared recognize.

Tonight was the engagement gala of Marco Bellini and Isabella Romano.

And Alessio was not here to celebrate.

The mask hid the scowl twisting his mouth as he scanned the room—gold-trimmed walls, white roses in tall crystal vases, Don Emilio seated at the far end like a spider in silk. Every face was smiling. Every smile was a lie.

He could feel the weight of it pressing against his ribs.

But there, across the room—like blood in a sea of porcelain—

She arrived.

Isabella stood beneath a crystal chandelier, wearing a dress the color of fresh wounds.

Blood-red silk hugged her curves, high slit, plunging neckline. Her back was bare, but her spine held steel.

Diamonds around her throat. The dagger Alessio gave her strapped to her thigh.

She didn't look like a bride-to-be.

She looked like a rebellion in heels.

Marco's hand rested on her waist, possessive, rehearsed. He leaned in and whispered something vile—a joke, probably.

She didn't hear it. Her eyes were locked on the masked man standing near the champagne tower.

Even behind the mask, she knew it was him.

The air shifted.

The chandelier above flickered once.

Her fingers curled against Marco's jacket as the music changed—slower, darker, a waltz laced with poison.

Alessio didn't approach.

But he didn't look away.

And neither did she.

The performance began.

A Game of Eyes and Glass

From opposite sides of the ballroom, they hunted each other with glances sharpened like stilettos.

Alessio leaned in the shadows of the marble archway, masked in black velvet and sin. The chandelier's fractured light caught the sharp angles of his suit, but not his face. His presence wasn't loud—it was inevitable.

Like a storm watching from the edge of a field, waiting for a single spark to justify its rage.

He didn't need to speak. He didn't need to move.

He only needed to watch her.

Isabella was spun across the floor by Marco Bellini, who smiled like a man convinced he owned her.

He touched her too casually, a hand too tight on her hip, lips brushing her ear as if proximity meant power.

But Alessio saw it—her spine locked, her jaw like stone behind the mask of civility.

She wore red. Not just any red. Blood-red. A shade that whispered rebellion. A statement, not a dress.

He smirked.
So she wants war too.

Across the room, her gaze slid to him.

Their eyes locked. A mistake. A challenge.

Time fractured.

In that suspended second, the gala blurred into irrelevance. The orchestra's strings turned to white noise. Conversations melted like candlewax.

Only one song played now—the one composed of heartbeat drums and glances too loaded to be innocent.

Isabella's POV:
She hated the way he looked at her.
Like he saw the seams in her skin. Like he already knew what she'd done with the dagger. What she was thinking when Marco touched her shoulder and she had to swallow the scream.

Alessio stood there, untouched by the gold and glitter of the evening. He didn't belong here—and yet he fit better than anyone. Danger wore him like a crown.

She hated that her body reacted before her mind caught up.

That her pulse stuttered. That her breath hitched when his eyes dropped—not to her dress, not to her lips, but to her thigh.

He knew.
Knew the dagger was there.
Knew it was meant for someone.

And his smirk—God, that smirk—was not a warning. It was permission.

She tore her eyes away first. Not because she was weak. But because the fire in her lungs told her she couldn't take more.

A waiter passed between them. Slipped a folded napkin into her palm. The motion was smooth, discreet. Practiced.

She didn't need to read it. She already knew.

"Cellar. Ten minutes."

She finished her dance. Marco's grip on her waist tightened as if sensing something slipping through his fingers.

"You look distant tonight," he murmured.

"I'm just trying to stay awake," she replied, sugar-sweet venom dripping off her tongue.

And when the music ended, she curtsied like a princess and walked straight into damnation.

The Cellar Confession

The cellar was built of stone and secrets.

Isabella pushed the heavy wooden door open and stepped into the cool dark. It smelled of wine and power—aged barrels, faded roses, and something older. Like memories buried alive.

Her heels clicked against the floor until she paused at the bottom of the steps, her breath caught halfway up her throat.

He was already there.

Alessio didn't speak right away. He emerged from the shadows like a punishment, dressed in that same dangerous black, the mask discarded now. What remained was the truth—carved into bone and wrapped in restraint.

She stared at him. He stared back. The silence between them stretched, pulled taut like a garrote.

"You came," he said.

"You knew I would."

He stepped closer. "And why is that, princess?"

She hated that the way he said it made her knees tremble. Not because he mocked her—but because he saw her. Saw the act. The façade. The girl with painted lips and bloody palms.

She lifted her chin. "Why are you here?"

"To remind you," he said, voice low and lethal, "that he doesn't own you."

Her heart slammed once against her ribs. "Neither do you."

"No," he said. "But I could."

She slapped him. The sound echoed against stone and steel.

He didn't flinch.

But then—his hand caught her wrist. Slow. Gentle. Terrifying.

His thumb brushed her pulse.

"You think I saved you in that garden because I wanted to play hero?"

"Didn't you?"

"No," he said, and stepped into her space. "I did it because I couldn't stomach the thought of him bruising something that's already mine."

"You're insane," she whispered, but her voice betrayed her.

"You haven't run."

Her breath hitched. "What happens if I stay?"

He didn't hesitate. "You're mine."

His hand tangled in her hair, the other pressing against the small of her back. He kissed her like it was a war he'd already won. No softness, no pretense. Just heat and fury and need.

Her mouth opened against his like a secret finally screamed.

She clawed at his jacket, pulled him closer. His tongue tasted like sin and sanctuary.

Her hands—fists now—shoved against his chest, not to push him away, but to anchor herself to something real.

Isabella's thoughts stung like fire:

This is madness. This is betrayal. This is everything I've never been allowed to want.

Alessio's thoughts sliced through like a blade:

Let her hate me. Let her damn me. But let her choose me, just once, in this darkness.

The kiss broke only when oxygen demanded it. Their breaths sawed between them. Foreheads pressed. Fingers still gripping like they'd fall if they let go.

"You don't get to choose for me," she whispered.

"No," he said. "But I can give you something they won't."

"What?"

"Power."

She stared at him, eyes wide. "What kind of power?"

"The kind that lets you decide what happens next."

He released her.

And it felt like a cliff edge.

She turned to leave—but paused, dagger still hidden, breath still shallow.

Behind her, his voice came, low and unholy.

"They'll try to break you."

She didn't turn back.
"I know."

"But if you fall," he said, "you fall into me."

She walked out into the gala of lies.

And above them, the orchestra played on.

But down in the cellar, something had already changed.

Not love.
Not yet.

But something older.
Something more dangerous.

A claim. A vow.

Because they didn't kiss like lovers.

They kissed like a war.

And neither of them would survive it clean.

CHAPTER 11

- The Unforgivable -

ALESSIO HAD ALWAYS known that desire had a cost. He just hadn't expected the bill to come so soon—or so bloody.

The moment his lips had left hers in that cellar, the moment her breath had hitched like confession against his skin, the world had already started to turn against them. Walls had mouths.

Enemies wore masks.

And every gilded corner of that cursed gala had ears tuned to betrayal.

It didn't take long.

By morning, word had slithered its way into Don Emilio's study like smoke through keyholes. The news came not as a whisper, but as an explosion.

The Romano princess had kissed the enemy.

And worse, the enemy had kissed her back.

It wasn't just disobedience. It was sacrilege.

Alessio stepped out of the back entrance of a warehouse near the docks, the early dawn wind cutting across his already-throbbing jaw.

The city was still asleep, but he knew better than to trust its silence. Silence, in his world, was the prelude to violence.

The first punch landed behind his right ear.

Then the second, square to the gut.

Four of them. Romano guards, dressed like dockworkers, their shoes too polished for the filth they pretended to stand in. Cowards sent by a coward.

He fought back like a man who had nothing left to lose—because in that moment, he didn't.

A cracked rib. Blood in his mouth. A broken wrist for one of them. A knee shattered beneath his boot. The sound of flesh meeting bone. The iron tang of fury.

He didn't run.

He made sure they did.

One limped away. One didn't get up.

The others would carry the message back to Don Emilio: Alessio Moretti may have kissed the girl, but he was still the devil they feared.

And devils didn't kneel.

They hunted.

The Warning from Within

It was near midnight when Salvatore found him again, leaning over the map table in the study with a bloodied shirt and fury tucked beneath his ribs like a second heartbeat.

The room smelled of scotch and old war.

"You're bleeding on the south docks," Salvatore said dryly.

Alessio didn't look up. "They started it."

Salvatore leaned against the doorway like a man preparing to witness a car crash. "You're losing your edge."

Alessio gave a humorless laugh. "Because I didn't kill all four?"

"Because you hesitated. Because you're letting her into your mind, into your decisions." Salvatore stepped closer.

"Don't pretend it's not happening. You think I haven't seen it before? That look in a man's eye when he's ready to trade kingdoms for a kiss?"

He poured a glass of whiskey, slid it across the table. "You've been sharp since the day you buried your father. Calculated. Cold. A weapon. And now—now you bleed for her."

Alessio stared at the map. At the red pins marking shipments. The blue ones tracking Romano movement. And the black X on Don Emilio's estate.

"I don't bleed for her," he said.

Salvatore raised a brow.

"I'd bleed *them* for her," Alessio clarified, voice dark as prophecy. "That's the difference."

His uncle was silent for a long moment, then muttered, "Jesus."

"No." Alessio's gaze lifted, steady. "Just the son of a dead man."

"You're spiraling."

"I'm choosing."

"You're choosing a girl who's been trained since birth to lie prettier than she smiles. She's a Romano. Don't forget that."

"I haven't," Alessio said, walking past him. "But I also haven't forgotten what it felt like to touch her skin and not want to wash my hands after."

And with that, he left the room.

He had a truth to deliver.

His Confession

The night air was thick with storm.

It hadn't broken yet, but it would. Alessio knew how to read tension in the sky the way he read it in a man's shoulders—something about to snap.

He waited in the northern gardens of the Romano estate, the only place without cameras, where stone statues whispered sins and rose thorns curved like fangs. He waited because she had come before. She always did.

And tonight, she did again.

She wore black. Not silk this time, but something more practical. He wondered if that meant she was preparing to run—or to fight.

Her eyes met his with a quiet fury. "What are you doing here?"

"I needed to see you."

She didn't move. "You shouldn't be here. Marco's already—"

"I know."

He stepped closer. The shadows swallowed most of his face, but his voice cut through like a blade. "I was ambushed. Four of your father's men."

Her breath hitched. "Are you—"

"I'm fine."

She shook her head. "You shouldn't have kissed me."

"You kissed me back."

"That doesn't mean anything."

"Then why are you here?"

Silence.

The roses behind her trembled in the wind.

"I need to tell you something," he said. "You deserve the

truth."

Her arms folded tightly across her chest, armor made of flesh. "What truth?"

He reached into his coat, pulling out a folded piece of paper. Yellowed, frayed at the edges. Her father's ledger.

"I found my father's journal," he said. "The last page... had a name circled in red."

He handed her the paper.

Her fingers took it slowly.

Then she saw it.

Emilio Romano.

"No," she whispered.

"Yes."

"You're lying."

"I wish I were."

She stared at the page like it might dissolve. Like if she blinked hard enough, it would change.

"That night," Alessio continued, voice rough, "your father ordered the hit. My father didn't die in a shootout. He was executed. Because he tried to pull out of an arms deal. Because he believed peace was possible."

She stumbled back.

He caught her by the wrist—not rough, just enough to ground her.

"I should hate you," he said. "You understand that? I should look at you and see only blood and betrayal. I should want to burn your family to ash and salt the grave."

"Then do it," she whispered, eyes glistening. "Hate me."

He stepped closer.

"I can't."

"Then kill me."

His hand rose to her face, brushing a strand of hair behind her ear like the act itself was sacred.

"I already did," he whispered.

And in that single sentence, the war between them cracked open wider than ever.

Because they both knew:

There are things worse than bullets.

Wounds sharper than betrayal.

And confessions that don't need forgiveness—only understanding.

Her world had always been stitched in lies, but tonight, truth was the blade.

And Alessio had buried it in her chest with the gentleness of a lover.

They stood in the dark—he, the heir of vengeance; she, the daughter of guilt.

And love?

Love was the gun left smoking on the ground between them.

Neither reached for it.

Because neither knew how to hold it without getting burned.

CHAPTER 12

- Hearts Don't Bleed -

THE SILENCE IN Isabella's room was not peaceful—it was feral. A living thing with teeth. It circled her like a wolf, licking its lips, daring her to cry out.

But she didn't.

Not when her father pounded on the door.

Not when her mother's soft, apologetic voice slithered through the cracks like smoke from a dying fire.

Not even when she looked in the mirror and saw a ghost in a red dress—a girl who used to obey, used to bend, used to believe in the mercy of men.

That girl was gone.

She had died in the cellar, beneath his mouth, beneath his promise: *If you stay, you're mine.*

And she had stayed.

Not for love. Not for lust.

But because something inside her had cracked wide open—and there was no going back.

The engagement was no longer just an arrangement. It was a coffin. And her father had already nailed the lid shut.

"You will marry Marco," he'd said that morning, his voice as cold and final as a tombstone. "There will be no discussion."

And that was the moment something inside her began to scream.

Now, in the middle of the night, she walked to her vanity with the grace of a condemned queen. She sat like a statue, unmoving, as her eyes studied the blade Alessio had given her.

The dagger—her grandmother's, stolen by the same family who now wanted to sell her like livestock.

She didn't flinch as she took it in her palm, the silver hilt biting into her skin like an oath. With one slow, deliberate motion, she pressed the blade to her hand and drew a line across her flesh.

Blood bloomed.

Not out of pain.

But defiance.

A silent scream in red.

She watched it drip. Crimson like her dress. Crimson like the rage curled in her chest.

It wasn't about him—Marco.

It wasn't even about Alessio.

It was about her.

And the woman she refused to lose again.

Letters Never Sent

The storm outside her window had died by morning, but inside her—there was only wreckage.

Isabella sat at her writing desk, pale fingers trembling over crisp parchment. The ink was already drying in crooked veins across the page, blotched where her tears had fallen without her permission. A silver fountain pen rested between her thumb and forefinger like a weapon far crueler than any blade.

Dear Alessio,
I wish I'd met you when the world was softer. Before blood became currency and love was a weakness branded in bone.
But we were born into kingdoms built on ash. You and I—flames pretending to be human.

She paused, breathing ragged, her ribs aching with every word that cost her more than she could afford. It was not the writing that hurt, but the realization that she would never send it.

Some truths belonged to silence, to paper folded and hidden behind secret panels, never reaching the hands that had burned her just enough to make her feel alive.

You make it impossible to breathe without needing more of you. I hate you for that. I hate myself more for letting it matter.

The page trembled as she gripped the edge, teeth clenched, ink smearing beneath her fingertips. She could almost see his face—etched in shadow, in firelight, in the echo of everything unsaid.

How cruel it was that the only man who ever saw her clearly was the one she was supposed to destroy.

But what did love mean in a house where loyalty came with a leash?

She folded the letter carefully, as if it were something sacred. No name on the envelope. No seal. Only the weight of a heart torn from its chest and pressed into lines that no one would read.

She placed it in the bottom drawer of her vanity, behind the box that held her mother's pearls—the same ones her father had gifted as an apology after the first broken promise.

This letter would join the others.

Unsent. Unspoken.

Unforgivable.

A Woman Reborn

The sun cracked through the horizon in violent hues of copper and bruised pink as Isabella stood at the mirror, the dagger Alessio had given her nestled beneath the silk sash at her hip. Her eyes—no longer glassy with grief, no longer blurred with fear—stared back at her like something ancient had awakened behind them.

She had always been porcelain—painted to be admired, fragile enough to be controlled. But porcelain, when shattered, became sharp.

She didn't wear white that morning.

White was the color of submission. Of pretty lies and women who obeyed.

Instead, she wore black—like mourning, like power, like an omen.

The household stirred as she walked down the corridor, her heels deliberate against the marble floors. Maids paused mid-step.

Guards straightened with wary glances. Even the tapestries lining the hall seemed to lean back from her path.

By the time she reached her father's study, her pulse was no longer erratic. It was thunder. Steady, certain.

She didn't knock.

The door burst open, and Don Emilio looked up from his desk with the expression of a man used to being feared.

Today, he would learn something new.

"I won't marry Marco," she said before he could speak.

His eyes narrowed. "You *will*—"

"No," she interrupted, voice like cold steel. "If you try to force me, I'll ruin us all. You've built this empire on secrets, lies, and silence. But I'm done playing by rules written in other people's blood."

Emilio stood slowly, face reddening, a storm darkening in his features. "You forget your place—"

"No," she said, and this time, she smiled—slow and dangerous. "I've just remembered it."

She stepped forward, placed a folded note on his desk. Her mother's handwriting. The last truth she'd ever been allowed to see.

A confession that Don Emilio had kept from her. One that tied her mother's death not to illness, but to betrayal.

"I know," she whispered. "About everything."

The silence cracked.

Her father sat down, suddenly unsure.

And Isabella turned her back to him—for the first time in her life.

She walked out without waiting for permission, the dagger warm against her thigh, her heart finally louder than her fear.

She wasn't a daughter anymore.

She was her own goddamn revolution.

Her voice didn't shake. Her dagger did not hide.

And as she walked away from the man who once owned her choices, Isabella Romano did not look back.

Because the girl who had once feared fire had learned to wield it.

And now—she was becoming it.

CHAPTER 13

- Smoke and Skin -

THERE WERE ASHES in her throat when she opened her eyes. Not literal—no, the fire hadn't reached her bedroom, not yet—but metaphorical, dream-wrought, heavy as sin. The memory of his voice clung to her skin like the silk sheets twisted around her legs.

"It was your blood. I should hate you."

He had said it like a benediction and a curse. A confession wrapped in a blade.

The air was still. Her room, too quiet. Something was missing. No—something had been replaced.

She sat up slowly, pulse skipping like a record in an old jukebox. Her fingers reached for the dagger beneath her pillow. The steel her rebellion had married. The symbol of her defiance.

It was gone.

In its place, resting atop the scarlet linen like a secret delivered in the night—

A single black rose.

Velvet-petaled. Deceptively soft. The kind of bloom that didn't grow in gardens, only in the hands of men who knew how to send messages without using words.

She didn't need to guess who had left it.

Isabella lifted the rose with a trembling hand. Pricks of thorn scraped her fingers, but she didn't bleed.

Not this time.

Because some wounds didn't spill crimson. Some sank deeper. Into the bone. Into the breath.

She stared at it, whispering the truth aloud—just once, so it wouldn't fester in her throat.

"He was here."

A Car Ride in Silence

He didn't text.

Didn't call.

Didn't ask permission.

Alessio Moretti simply arrived—like storm clouds rolling over the sea. His black car idled at the edge of the estate driveway, polished like onyx, windows tinted as dark as his eyes.

She knew it was him the second her bare feet hit the marble foyer.

No driver stepped out. No guard announced him. There were no theatrics. No flash of violence. Just… gravity.

Something about him pulled. Always had.

When she opened the car door, the scent of leather and smoke greeted her like an old lover.

He didn't look at her right away.

His hands rested on the steering wheel like they could kill or cradle. He wore all black—tailored to his fury, silence sewn into every seam.

She slid into the passenger seat without speaking.

He pulled away.

No destination offered.

No words spoken.

Just the road stretching before them like a knife edge, slicing through the quiet.

But silence with Alessio was never empty.

It was loaded.

His thigh brushed hers when they turned. She felt the weight of his gaze when she looked out the window. His hand flexed on the gearshift every time she exhaled too sharply.

The tension was not accidental.

It was foreplay disguised as stillness.

And when they stopped—fifteen minutes later in front of a glass high-rise that touched the clouds—Isabella wasn't sure if her heart was racing from fear… or desire.

Probably both.

The Apartment

She followed him up in silence, carried by a private elevator with no buttons. Just a key he turned at the top.

A private floor. A penthouse. Alessio Moretti's world—untouched, unseen.

He stepped aside to let her in first, like a gentleman hiding a wolf under his skin.

The space was steel and stone. Glass walls offering views of a city that never blinked. A bar stocked with crystal decanters. A fireplace already burning, as if it had known she was coming.

She stood at the edge of his territory like prey pretending not to be.

"This is where you live?" she asked softly, unsure why it

mattered.

"No." His voice was low. "This is where I burn."

He walked past her, shedding his coat, tossing it onto a velvet chair. There was no attempt to charm, no seduction draped in sweet nothings.

Just heat.

And hunger.

And something unspoken between them that pulsed like a live wire.

He poured a drink.

She wandered toward the floor-to-ceiling windows. The city glittered below like shattered promises.

"How many women have been here?" she asked.

He didn't lie.

"One. And she's standing in front of my window."

She turned.

He was closer than before.

She didn't move back.

Not this time.

A Slow-Burn Spicy Moment

The city glowed beneath them, a mosaic of burning windows and secrets no one would admit. Alessio said nothing as he poured two glasses of whiskey, the amber catching fire in the dim light.

He handed her one, their fingers brushing for the briefest second—yet it felt like friction, like silk dragged across flame.

"I didn't bring you here to seduce you," he said, voice low and sharp.

"I know," she replied.

But her voice betrayed her. It trembled—not with fear, but with anticipation. Her body already knew something her mind hadn't caught up to yet.

The silence between them stretched, heavy and aching, the kind that begged to be broken by breath and skin.

She stepped toward the glass wall, her reflection merging with the skyline. She didn't know if she was admiring the view or running from him. From herself.

He came up behind her—not touching, just near. Close enough that she could feel the tension radiating off his body like a second skin. Close enough that the air between them was no longer breathable.

"You're afraid of me," he murmured, voice grazing her nape.

"I'm afraid of what I feel around you."

He didn't move. Didn't press.
Only said, "Tell me to stop."

She turned to him then—slowly, like surrender could be graceful if done right. Her lips parted, but no words came. Just breath. Just want.

"I can't," she whispered.
That was all he needed.

He reached for her—slow, deliberate, reverent. His hand settled on her jaw, thumb tracing the curve of her cheek.

It wasn't hunger. It wasn't even lust. It was possession wrapped in reverence.

"Then remember," he said, tone iron wrapped in velvet, "you wanted this before I even kissed you."

His mouth found hers in the quiet.
No crash. No violence.
Just a promise.

A kiss that pressed into the wound and sealed it with heat.

His hands didn't roam greedily. They claimed territory like a man who knew he'd already won the war but craved the battle anyway. Her fingers tangled in his shirt, dragging him closer, until her back met the glass wall and the city lights watched.

His lips moved from her mouth to the line of her jaw, to the column of her neck, tasting defiance and despair in equal measure. When he kissed the hollow of her throat, her knees nearly buckled.

He caught her.

"Alessio…" she breathed, but it wasn't a protest. It was a prayer.

He kissed her collarbone like he was branding it. One hand anchored at her waist, the other sliding up her spine—slow, never rushed. When his fingers brushed the zipper of her dress, he paused.

She didn't flinch.

Instead, she took his hand and pressed it against her chest—where her heart raced like a trapped animal.

"You feel that?" she whispered.

His eyes darkened. "That's mine now."

The zipper didn't fall.
Her dress stayed on, so did his control. Barely.

But his mouth worshipped every inch of exposed skin like she was a cathedral he hadn't believed in until now.

They didn't speak for hours.

Not because there was nothing to say, but because everything worth saying was already carved into the silence between them. Alessio sat beside her on the bed—not touching her, not pushing.

Just there.

A presence. A shadow. A storm tamed only by her breath.

She leaned into him slowly, head resting against his shoulder, letting the silence be an answer. His arm came around her without fanfare.

She felt the weight of it—strong, steady, absolute.

He didn't ask her to stay. She didn't ask to leave.
They simply existed there—two people circling the edge of ruin.

At some point, her eyes closed.

Not from exhaustion, but because for the first time, she didn't feel like she had to keep watching her back. Not here. Not with him.

Alessio's breath stirred her hair.

His lips brushed her temple—not a kiss, not quite.
More like a promise with no words.

He didn't take her that night.

He could have.
She would've let him.

But instead, he just held her.
Like a man holding the thing he never thought he deserved.

And maybe that was what made it more dangerous than anything else.

Because this wasn't just tension.

This was beginning to look like trust.

Like belonging.

And Isabella, for all her fire, had never known what it meant to be touched like a secret instead of a possession.

As the city dimmed beneath them and shadows crept across the skyline, she knew one thing:

He didn't own her body.

But he was starting to own her silence.

And silence—when willingly given—was the most sacred thing she'd ever offered anyone.

CHAPTER 14

- The Rules of Wanting -

THE AIR IN THE room felt colder than usual, but Alessio's blood ran hot.

He sat at the long mahogany table in his private meeting room, eyes pinned to the files spread before him—intel on Romano movements, gun shipments rerouted, Marco's face circled in red.

Don Emilio's ledger had become a battlefield of ink and blood.

Across from him, Enzo—his consigliere since he was sixteen—leaned forward.

"You're slipping," Enzo said, voice quiet, but firm. "The men are talking. They say your hands shake when her name is mentioned."

Alessio didn't flinch. "Then they're liars."

"You haven't touched the Marco situation. You haven't retaliated against the Romano docks. You've been... distracted."

Alessio folded the file closed like he was sealing a coffin. "Isabella Romano has nothing to do with my decisions."

A pause. Then:

"Then why is her dress in your penthouse closet?" Enzo asked.

Alessio's jaw ticked. That crimson scrap of silk—left behind from the gala—had become a wound that refused to close. Every time he opened the closet, he saw it. Her. A memory sewn in red.

"I handle threats with precision," Alessio said, rising. "Even the beautiful ones."

"You say that like it's not already too late."

Alessio walked to the bar, poured himself a drink, didn't answer.

Because it *was* too late.

His lies were clean. But his fists were bleeding. From the bag he punched every night trying to forget how her lips tasted when she trembled.

He didn't sleep. Didn't eat much. Just trained. Planned. And waited for her to come back—to test him again.

And when she did, he'd remember the rules he never voiced.

Because wanting her wasn't the problem.

It was needing her that would destroy everything.

She arrived in silence.

No knock. No grand entrance. Just the sound of her boots on gravel and the sudden hush of the training yard.

Alessio looked up from the targets he'd been demolishing all morning. And there she was.

Wearing black denim, a fitted leather jacket, and fire in her eyes.

"I want you to teach me," she said.

He didn't have to ask what.

He tossed her a Glock. "Then let's see if you're ready to stop being the prey."

She caught it without hesitation.

And for the next hour, the world narrowed to just them.

He moved behind her, correcting her grip, his hands ghosting over her hips. Each touch was calculated, but each one cost him. Her scent curled into his lungs like smoke. Her heartbeat, steady against his chest, tempted his control.

"Breathe with it," he murmured into her ear, as she aimed. "The gun isn't an enemy. It's a conversation."

She fired. Missed.

He adjusted her again, closer this time. His palm flattened against her lower back. Her head tilted—just enough to brush his jaw.

"You're thinking about me," she whispered.

"I always do," he admitted, raw.

She turned. The Glock dangled from her hand like a forgotten thought.

He took it from her fingers.

And placed it aside.

A Line Crossed

"I shouldn't want this," she said, eyes locked to his.

"But you do."

"I shouldn't want you."

"But you do."

He stepped forward, slow, deliberate. Like a man walking into the mouth of his own death.

She didn't step back.

"I told you once," he murmured, "I don't have a heart."

"And I told you once," she said, voice like silk cutting skin, "neither do I."

Then she moved first.

Her lips crashed against his like fury unleashed. He answered her with hands on her hips, mouth claiming, devouring, begging without words.

She straddled him on the edge of the shooting bench, thighs framing his, gun forgotten on the floor.

He groaned her name—not in pain.

In *surrender.*

One hand buried in her hair. The other beneath her jacket, skimming skin, memorizing every inch.

But still—they held back. They danced at the edge of a cliff they weren't ready to jump from.

He kissed her like she was the sin he'd never confess to.

She kissed him like she'd already forgiven herself.

It wasn't the gun that made her dangerous.

It was the way she looked at him after pulling the trigger—like she had finally tasted power, and now, nothing could ever feed her the same again.

She stood with the stance of a goddess reborn, smoke curling off the barrel, lips parted not in fear but exhilaration. Alessio hadn't breathed since she hit the bullseye.

His heart didn't beat—it staggered. And then she turned, slow, deliberate, walking toward him like the room belonged to her now.

She stopped in front of him. Close. Too close.

Her voice was low, almost teasing. "Did I pass?"

He didn't answer. Couldn't.

Not when she was looking at him like that.

Not when his control was a thread already fraying.

His hand reached for the pistol still resting on the bench, but it wasn't about the weapon anymore. It was about grounding himself.

Remembering who he was before her—before that damn red dress, before the defiance in her eyes and the softness in her mouth ruined everything he thought he knew about discipline.

Isabella stepped between his legs and straddled the bench, one knee sliding to either side of him.

Her skirt hiked up just enough to reveal the satin holster he'd given her, still snug against her thigh.

It should've been a warning. Instead, it made his pulse spike.

"Careful," he murmured, voice dark with restraint. "You're playing with fire."

She leaned in, her mouth inches from his. "Maybe I want to burn."

The sound he made wasn't quite a groan—it was surrender cut with hunger. He reached for her, hands gripping her hips, guiding her down until she was fully seated in his lap.

Her breath hitched, just once, and his control broke cleanly down the middle.

He tilted his head up, brushing his lips across her jawline, not kissing—*memorizing*. His mouth lingered beneath her ear, his voice little more than a growl.

"I warned you," he said.

"Warn me again," she whispered, her fingers curling into his shirt like she wanted to tear the fabric and the man from the seams.

And so he did.

He warned her with his mouth against her throat, with his hand fisted in her hair, with the brutal tenderness of a man who had spent his life starving and just discovered what it meant to taste.

Her fingers traced the scar at his temple, and he let her—for the first time, he let someone touch the broken part of him without flinching.

They didn't undress.

They didn't need to.

Because this wasn't about sex—not yet.

It was about *wanting* so badly, it hurt. It was the kind of hunger that fed on patience, that begged to be stretched, drawn out, made sacred through restraint.

Every kiss he gave her was a vow. Every sigh she spilled against his neck was a sin he never wanted absolved.

And when she whispered his name—not like a question, not like a threat, but like it *belonged* to her—Alessio moaned for the first time.

Not in pain.

In surrender.

He pressed his forehead to hers, breath ragged. "You undo me."

She smiled, wrecked and radiant. "Good."

He kissed her again, slow and deep, until time forgot how to move.

When he finally pulled away—barely, barely—her lips were swollen, her fingers still trembling against his chest.

Alessio looked at her like she was the last line between him and damnation. Maybe she was.

"If you leave now," he said, voice raw, "I'll let you go."

The room stilled. Her eyes met his.

She didn't move.

She didn't speak.

She simply *stayed*—her silence louder than any yes, her body choosing him the way no words ever could.

And in that stillness, Alessio understood something he hadn't before:

He could survive war.

He could survive betrayal, loss, blood.

But he wouldn't survive *losing her*.

Not again.

Not ever.

So when she kissed him this time—slow, reverent, with the quiet desperation of two people rewriting fate—he let himself believe in something impossible.

Hope.

And maybe that was the most dangerous thing of all.

CHAPTER 15

- The Longest Night -

THE AIR BETWEEN them wasn't empty. It was loaded—heavy like the barrel of a gun cocked with truths they hadn't dared speak.

She sat in his penthouse kitchen, wearing one of his shirts, sleeves rolled to her elbows. The hem danced around her thighs like a secret. The silver fork in her hand trembled, not from fear—but from restraint.

She'd been burning ever since the night at the range, and now, the match that was Alessio sat across from her, refusing to strike.

He didn't eat. Just watched.

Watched the curve of her jaw, the ghost of a smile she wore like armor. Watched the way her eyes never stayed on him long enough—like looking too long might ruin them both.

Isabella cut her chicken into even pieces she wouldn't eat. "You're quiet."

"I'm thinking."

"Dangerous," she murmured, glancing at him. "For whom?"

He didn't answer. His thumb rubbed the edge of his whiskey glass like it was her skin. His silence was an entire language. And tonight, he was fluent in denial.

The tension swirled in their shared air, dense with everything unsaid: the kiss in the cellar, the gun in her hand, the way he had worshipped her without ever touching her fully.

There was thunder outside. Rain began to fall, slow at first, like hesitant fingers on glass. Then harder—wild and relentless. Nature's warning.

A second later, the power went out.

The lights died. The hum of the refrigerator cut out. The air conditioner exhaled its final breath.

Silence.

Only rain.

And two hearts beginning to pound too loudly in the dark.

Isabella's Perspective

The sudden darkness enveloped them, the only illumination the soft flicker of a single candle. The storm outside mirrored the turmoil within her—a tempest of desire and uncertainty.

She could feel Alessio's gaze upon her, heavy and expectant, yet he remained silent, as if waiting for her to bridge the chasm between them.

The rain intensified, its rhythmic patter against the windows a soothing contrast to the pounding of her heart. She longed to reach out, to close the distance, but fear held her captive. Fear of rejection, fear of the unknown, fear of the consequences of surrendering to the magnetic pull between them.

Alessio's Perspective

The candlelight danced in her eyes, reflecting the storm's fury outside. He watched her, captivated by her beauty and the vulnerability she tried so hard to conceal.

Every instinct screamed to take her in his arms, to claim her as his own, but he resisted.

This was not just about physical desire; it was about trust, about breaking down the walls they had both so carefully constructed.

The rain outside was a metaphor for his own emotions—uncontrolled, overwhelming, and threatening to flood the carefully dammed barriers he had built around his heart.

He needed her, more than he had ever needed anyone, yet he feared what that need might cost them both.

Isabella's Perspective

She couldn't remember who moved first—whether it was him leaning in or her closing the gap between them. All she knew was that their lips met in a kiss that was both tentative and desperate, as if they were both afraid of what would happen if they stopped.

His hands were gentle as they cupped her face, thumbs brushing over her cheeks, memorizing the feel of her skin. She responded in kind, her fingers threading through his hair, pulling him closer, deepening the kiss.

When they finally broke apart, breathless and yearning, she whispered, "Stay with me."

He didn't speak, but his actions spoke volumes. He stood, extending a hand to her, his eyes dark with unspoken promises.

She took his hand, allowing him to lead her to the bedroom, where the world outside ceased to exist.

There were no words as he undressed her, each piece of clothing falling away like a layer of armor she hadn't realized she was wearing.

His touch was reverent, as if she were something precious, something he had longed for but never dared to touch.

He paused at a scar on her thigh, his fingers tracing its outline.

"This?" he murmured, "It belongs to me now."

Her breath hitched at his words, a mixture of surprise and something deeper stirring within her. She nodded, unable to trust her voice.

He kissed the scar softly, then met her gaze. "You're mine, Isabella. In every way that matters."

The weight of his words settled over her, and for the first time, she felt truly seen, truly claimed.

She responded in kind, her hands exploring his body, learning the feel of him, memorizing the planes and muscles that defined him.

They moved together, a dance as old as time, each seeking solace in the other's embrace. The world outside ceased to exist; there was only the two of them, lost in a moment that felt both timeless and fleeting.

When they finally collapsed together, tangled in sheets and each other, she rested her head on his chest, listening to the steady beat of his heart.

Alessio's Perspective

He had been with many women, but none had ever affected him the way Isabella did. Her touch ignited something within him, something he had long buried under layers of indifference and control.

As they lay together, he traced patterns on her back, memorizing the feel of her skin beneath his fingertips.

He wanted to say something, to express the torrent of emotions swirling within him, but words failed him.

Instead, he kissed her forehead, a silent promise that he would protect her, cherish her, and never let her go.

Isabella's Perspective

His eyes never left hers as he slowly undressed her, each movement deliberate, each piece of clothing removed with reverence. She felt exposed, vulnerable, yet strangely empowered under his gaze.

When he reached the scar on her thigh, he paused, his fingers tracing its outline.

"This?" he asked, his voice husky with desire. "It belongs to me now."

She nodded, her breath catching in her throat. His lips met the scar, soft and lingering, branding her with his touch.

Alessio's Perspective

Her skin was a map he wanted to explore, each scar, each mark telling a story he longed to understand. As he kissed the scar on her thigh, he felt a possessiveness surge within him, a need to claim her in every sense.

"You're mine," he whispered against her skin, "in every way that matters."

Isabella's Perspective

The initial nervousness melted away as they moved together, their bodies finding a rhythm, a connection that transcended words. In his arms, she felt safe, cherished, and desired.

Alessio's Perspective

For the first time in years, he allowed himself to be vulnerable, to let go of the walls he had built around his heart.

With Isabella, he found a sanctuary, a place where he could be himself without fear of judgment or rejection.

They didn't sleep. Not because of desire. But because neither wanted to forget what it felt like to belong—even for one night.

CHAPTER 16

- Blood and Bedsheets -

THERE ARE MOMENTS that exist outside of time.
This was one of them, the sun hadn't yet broken the skyline, but the room was already steeped in shadows, the kind that clung to flesh and didn't let go.

Alessio lay still, the sheets tangled around his hips, his bare chest rising and falling beneath the weight of her breath against it.

Isabella slept with one hand splayed across his ribs, as if anchoring herself to something real. Her hair was a dark river across his skin, a waterfall of warmth and softness no bullet could replicate, no war could excuse.

He studied her—not with a soldier's eye, but with something far more dangerous.

A man's heart.

And in the quiet ache of morning, Alessio Moretti did something reckless.
He allowed himself to feel.

He didn't deserve her. But gods didn't always ask permission when they handed down fire to mortals. They just watched the burn.

His fingers brushed her shoulder, then paused at the scar

beneath her collarbone. A token of pain. A memory someone else had given her.

He kissed it—soft, reverent. Not to claim it. But to mourn it.

She stirred.

"Mmm," her voice was soft silk. "You're watching me."

"I always am."

Her lashes fluttered, then slowly, she opened her eyes—stormy with sleep, unreadable and vulnerable and beautiful in a way that hurt. The kind of beauty that made men kill.

Or forgive. He wasn't sure which one he'd do first if someone tried to take her from him again.

"You didn't sleep," she murmured.

"No." He didn't explain. Couldn't.

Because how did you explain the kind of night where skin met skin and didn't lie—where truth wasn't spoken, only breathed into collarbones and echoed in the small, sacred space between bodies?

She sat up slowly, the sheet falling, revealing bruises not from pain—but from pleasure. His mouth had left those. And the fire in his gut returned, hungry and guilt-ridden.

He should leave, but he didn't.

Couldn't.

Instead, he leaned in and said the only thing he could in the quiet:
"I shouldn't want you like this."

She tilted her head, eyes unblinking. "But you do."

God help him. He nodded.

Interrupted Bliss

The ringtone shattered the moment.

Alessio's muscles tightened like a noose. He reached for the phone without looking. Only one number had that tone—direct from Enzo, his second-in-command. It only rang for blood.

"Talk," he barked, voice still hoarse from sleep—or something more tender.

Enzo's voice came cold and clipped: "Marco's been spotted. Our docks. North side."

Alessio's heart cracked in half.

He stood, the sheets falling to the floor, and walked to the window like a man sentenced to death. Below, the city pulsed with early-morning hunger. But his world—the real world—was already bleeding.

"You want eyes on him?" Enzo asked.

"No," Alessio growled. "I want blood."

Behind him, Isabella had wrapped herself in a blanket. She didn't ask questions. Didn't need to. She knew what it meant when a man like Alessio dressed in silence.

Her voice was steady, but her hands trembled. "You have to go."

He stopped. Turned.

There it was again. That unbearable thing. Not just want—but *care*. She was scared *for* him. Not *of* him.

He closed the distance between them and cradled her face in his hands. "I'll come back," he said. A promise. A curse.

"Don't," she whispered. "Don't make promises in a world like this."

He kissed her anyway. Not because he disagreed—but because he already knew he wasn't coming back whole.

Blood Spilled

The docks greeted Alessio with their usual symphony of

creaks and groans, the wooden planks slick with the remnants of a passing storm.

The air was thick with the scent of salt and decay, a fitting backdrop for the carnage that awaited him.

Enzo met him at the entrance of the warehouse, his face a mask of controlled fury.

"They were swift," he reported, his voice tight.

"Infiltrated our ranks with the precision of ghosts. Three of ours lie cold, Matteo among them."

Alessio's gaze hardened as he stepped over the threshold, his boots leaving imprints in the pooling blood. The sight of his fallen men, their lifeless eyes staring into the abyss, ignited a furnace of rage within him.

Each body told a story of interrupted futures, of families torn asunder, of promises unfulfilled.

He knelt beside Matteo, his fingers brushing the young man's hand, still warm but slipping away into the eternal night. Matteo had been more than a soldier; he had been a brother, a son, a dreamer with aspirations beyond the underworld's grasp.

Now, he was a casualty in a war that devoured the innocent with equal fervor.

Alessio's breath came in shallow gasps as he surveyed the scene, his mind racing to piece together the puzzle.

The precision of the attack spoke of intimate knowledge, of betrayal from within.

But it was the message left behind that gnawed at his insides—a grotesque signature carved into the flesh of one of his men.

"We see you. We see her."

The words were simple, yet they carried the weight of a thousand threats. They were no longer just challenging his authority; they were encroaching upon his personal sanctum, threatening the woman who had become his anchor in a world devoid of stability.

His hand clenched into a fist, the urge to strike something, anything, overwhelming him.

Enzo placed a steadying hand on his shoulder, a silent acknowledgment of the tempest raging within him.

"We'll find them," Enzo vowed, his voice low and unwavering.

"And when we do, there will be no mercy."

Alessio nodded, his eyes scanning the room, taking in every detail, every shadow that might conceal an enemy.

"Prepare the men," he ordered, his voice cold and devoid of emotion.

"Tonight, we send a message of our own."

The journey back to the city was a blur, the rhythmic thrum of the engine doing little to calm Alessio's turbulent thoughts. His mind replayed the events at the docks—the faces of the fallen, the chilling message, the gnawing fear for Isabella's safety.

Each thought was a shard of glass, cutting deeper into his resolve.

He bypassed the compound, bypassed the usual channels, driven by an instinct he couldn't name but couldn't ignore. His only thought was to reach her, to ensure she was untouched by the storm that was about to engulf his world.

He entered his apartment quietly, the familiar surroundings offering little comfort.

The soft glow of the bedside lamp illuminated the figure seated on his bed, her silhouette a beacon in the encroaching darkness.

Isabella looked up as he entered, her expression a mixture

of concern and determination. Without a word, she rose and crossed the room, her arms enveloping him in a warmth he desperately needed but didn't deserve.

"They know," he murmured against her hair, his voice rough. "They've crossed a line."

She pulled back slightly, her hands cupping his face, her eyes searching his for answers.

"Then we fight back," she said, her voice steady, unwavering.

He shook his head, a bitter laugh escaping him. "It's not that simple. This is a war, Isabella. And you're now a target."

Her gaze never wavered. "I've always been a target, Alessio. But I've chosen this path, chosen you. And I won't run from it now."

Her words, simple yet profound, struck him with the force of a revelation. She was no longer the woman he had to protect; she was his equal, his partner in this dance of shadows and blood.

He kissed her then, not with the desperation of a man clinging to the last vestiges of his humanity, but with the certainty of one who had found his other half in a world that offered none.

As they parted, he rested his forehead against hers, his breath mingling with hers.

"Stay with me," he whispered, the plea evident in his tone.

"Always," she replied, her arms tightening around him.

And in that moment, amidst the chaos and the bloodshed, amidst the enemies closing in and the world crumbling around them, Alessio Moretti found a semblance of peace.

Not because the storm had passed, but because he no longer faced it alone.

CHAPTER 17

- Her Father's Eyes -

POV: Isabella

THE CLINK OF silver against porcelain echoed in the dimly lit dining room as I set the last plate on the table.

The aroma of roasted lamb mingled with the faint scent of jasmine from the garden, but neither could mask the tension that hung heavier than any perfume.

Father sat at the head of the table, his eyes not on the food but on me, as if measuring my every movement, every breath. His gaze was a weight I had borne since childhood, a constant reminder of expectations unspoken yet deeply felt.

"Sit," he commanded, his voice low, carrying the authority that had shaped my existence.

I obeyed, lowering myself into the chair opposite him. The silence stretched between us, thick and suffocating, until he finally spoke, his words deliberate, each syllable a stone dropped into the stillness.

"You're going to marry Marco in one week," he announced, his eyes never leaving mine.

"It's final."

The world seemed to tilt, the room spinning as his words sank in. Marco. The name alone sent a shiver down my spine. He was a man of the underworld, his reputation built on whispers and shadows. And now, he was to be my husband.

"But Father," I began, my voice trembling, "I—"

He raised a hand, silencing me. "No arguments. This is not up for discussion."

Panic surged within me, my heart pounding against my ribs as if trying to escape. The walls of the room seemed to close in, the air thick with the scent of impending doom.

"Father, please," I pleaded, my voice breaking, "I don't want this. I don't want him."

His eyes hardened, his expression unwavering. "You will do as you're told. Disobedience will not be tolerated."

The room felt colder now, the warmth of the meal forgotten. I pushed my plate away, the food suddenly unappetizing.

"Father," I whispered, my voice barely audible, "I love someone else."

His gaze flickered, a fleeting moment of something—anger, perhaps, or disappointment—before he masked it with a cold indifference.

"Your feelings are irrelevant," he said flatly. "This marriage will strengthen our position. It's not about love."

Tears welled in my eyes, blurring my vision. I had always known my life was not my own, that duty and family came first. But this? This was a betrayal of everything I had ever hoped for.

I stood abruptly, the chair scraping against the floor, and fled the room, my father's voice calling after me, but I couldn't stop. I couldn't breathe.

I ran through the halls, down the stairs, out into the night, the cool air a sharp contrast to the fire raging within me.

The moon hung low, casting long shadows as I collapsed onto the garden bench, my body wracked with sobs.

I thought of Alessio—his touch, his warmth, the way he made me feel seen, truly seen.

And now, it was all slipping away, torn from me by the very man who had given me life.

I remembered his hands, strong and gentle, his lips that spoke words of comfort and passion. I remembered the safety I felt in his arms, a safety that now seemed like a distant dream.

The pain was unbearable, a crushing weight on my chest. I screamed into the night, the sound raw and primal, a release of all the fear, the anger, the grief that consumed me.

And then, amidst the chaos of my thoughts, a resolve began to form.

I couldn't accept this. I couldn't let my father dictate my life, my happiness.

I would fight.

The days that followed were a blur of preparations and hollow smiles. I moved through the motions, a puppet in a play I had no desire to be part of.

Each fitting, each meeting with Marco felt like a betrayal to myself, to the love I had found in Alessio.

But beneath the surface, the rebellion I had ignited in my heart burned brighter each day. I began to seek out allies, those who might help me escape this fate.

I learned of women who had broken free from the chains of arranged marriages, who had found freedom and safety. Their stories fueled my determination.

I met with Father Luigi Ciotti, a priest known for aiding women escaping the mafia's grip.

His eyes, kind yet filled with sorrow, listened as I poured out my fears and hopes.

"We will find a way," he assured me, his voice steady.

"You are not alone."

And so, the plan began to form. A network of safe houses, forged identities, and a route to freedom.

But it was dangerous, fraught with risks that could cost us everything.

The night before the wedding, I stood before the mirror, staring at the reflection of the woman I was supposed to be. The dress, white and pure, mocked me with its symbolism.

I was not pure; I was broken, shattered by the weight of expectations and the chains of my family's legacy.

A knock at the door startled me, and I turned to see Alessio standing there, his presence a balm to my wounded soul.

"Isabella," he whispered, crossing the room to take my hands in his.

"I couldn't let you go through with this."

Tears filled my eyes as I looked into his familiar, comforting eyes.

"I can't marry him, Alessio. I can't betray us."

He cupped my face, his touch grounding me. "Then don't. Come with me. We can start over, leave all this behind."

The fear was still there, gnawing at the edges of my resolve. But with Alessio, there was hope, a flicker of light in the darkness.

"We'll fight them together," he vowed, his voice fierce with determination.

And so, we did.

"He wants to break you," Alessio whispered when she returned.

"Then we break him first," she replied, voice shaking. And so it began.

CHAPTER 18

- The Pact of No Return -

THE RAIN HAD stopped by the time Alessio arrived at the abandoned chapel on the outskirts of Valmonti.

His boots echoed against cracked marble. Dust shimmered in the air like ash from an old fire. The pews were long gone, the altar forgotten.

But he wasn't here to pray. He was here to strike a deal with the only devil who might save them.

Isabella stood near the altar, draped in black. Her hair was loose. Her hands bare. She didn't flinch when he stepped closer. They had run out of fear to flinch from.

"You're late," she said softly.

"I needed to be sure we weren't followed."

Their eyes met—war-tired, rage-sharpened. It wasn't the first time they'd stood at a crossroads. But it was the first time the path behind them had truly disappeared.

He pulled a folded paper from his coat—an old map of the Romanos' dock shipment routes.

"I spoke to Nicolo. He'll feed Marco a lie. Say I want a truce. Offer him a temporary alliance. We pretend to stand down. Get close. Then—"

"Then we kill him." Her voice didn't waver.

Alessio stared at her, his breath held. Not because of the blood she was willing to spill. But because she no longer asked who would pay for it.

He walked to her slowly, pressing the map between her palms.

"And your father?"

Her jaw clenched. "He dies, too."

A beat of silence passed. Not hesitation—calculation.

"Once Marco's dead, Emilio's exposed. He won't survive the blowback."

Alessio nodded. "Then we strike twice. First the fiancé. Then the father."

And so the pact was born—not from hope, but from hunger.

The Pact

They returned to his car. Rain began again—soft, like the world was mourning something it couldn't name.

Inside, Alessio's hands gripped the steering wheel tight. Not because of fear, but because she was so close now. Because this woman beside him, once a pawn, now held kingdoms in her stare.

"We'll tell your father I'm stepping down," Alessio said. "That I want peace. I'll toast your engagement in front of a hundred liars. And behind every smile, I'll count the seconds until I slit Marco's throat."

She turned to him, her voice low. "And I'll kiss Marco on the cheek. Smile like I'm the obedient daughter. Then I'll hand him the knife you'll use."

He looked at her then—not like a lover, but like a comrade. She was beautiful, yes. But it was the fire beneath her skin that made him ache. She wasn't his queen.

She was his executioner.

"We lie to everyone," she said, turning her palm up between them. "We betray everyone. Together."

His hand met hers.

"And we don't come back from this," she added.

"No," he agreed. "We don't."

They didn't go back to the city.

Instead, Alessio drove them to the countryside, to a villa surrounded by vineyards that had long grown wild. It had once belonged to his mother's side—before blood had stained the family name.

Now, it was forgotten land. Sacred in its silence.

There were no guards. No plans. No war waiting in the next room.

Just the soft creak of floorboards, the smell of old wood and lavender, and the kind of night that only comes before everything burns.

He lit a single fire in the hearth.

She stood at the window, arms crossed. The moonlight painted her silver.

When she spoke, it was barely audible. "Will you still want me after this?"

He came up behind her, hands on her hips, lips at her ear.

"I wanted you before I knew your name. I'll want you long after they curse it."

Her body turned toward him. No rush. No fire—yet. Just inevitability.

Their kiss wasn't urgent this time.

It was reverent.

Like a promise made flesh.

The villa's ancient timbers groaned under the weight of the storm outside, but inside, the world was reduced to the two of them—a man and a woman bound by blood, ambition, and an undeniable, simmering attraction.

Isabella stood before Alessio, her silhouette framed by the flickering firelight.

The shadows danced across her features, highlighting the determination in her eyes and the subtle vulnerability that lurked beneath her fierce exterior.

She reached for the hem of her black dress, lifting it slowly, deliberately, revealing the smooth expanse of her legs.

Alessio's breath hitched, his gaze following every movement, every inch of exposed skin.

She stepped closer, her presence enveloping him, her scent—a heady mix of jasmine and something uniquely her own—filling his senses.

Her fingers traced the line of his jaw, sending a shiver down his spine.

"Is this what you want, Alessio?" she whispered, her voice a melodic blend of challenge and invitation.

Without a word, he pulled her into his arms, capturing her lips in a kiss that was both desperate and tender. The taste of her was intoxicating, a blend of wine and something sweeter, something that belonged only to her.

His hands roamed to her back, unclasping the delicate fabric, letting it fall to the floor in a pool of silk.

Isabella was unadorned now, save for the firelight that painted her skin in warm hues. She met his gaze, her eyes dark with desire, her breath shallow.

"Touch me, Alessio," she murmured.

He obliged, his hands exploring, memorizing the feel of her—soft curves, the dip of her waist, the swell of her breasts.

She arched into him, a soft gasp escaping her lips as his fingers brushed against her sensitive skin.

Their movements were a dance, a rhythm they had unknowingly rehearsed, each touch, each caress, a silent promise of what was to come.

Clothes became a distant memory, discarded carelessly as they sought the warmth of each other's skin.

Isabella straddled him, her hands braced on his chest, her hair cascading around them like a dark halo.

She moved with a slow, deliberate pace, each roll of her hips eliciting a groan from Alessio, each movement a testament to the fire that burned between them.

"Say my name," he rasped, his hands gripping her hips, guiding her movements.

She leaned down, her lips brushing against his ear, her breath hot against his skin.

"Alessio," she breathed, her voice laced with passion and something deeper—something unspoken.

The sound of her saying his name, like a prayer, sent him spiraling, his control slipping, unraveling with each passing second.

He flipped them over, pinning her beneath him, his lips trailing a path down her neck, tasting, marking, claiming.

Their bodies moved in a frenzy, a blur of motion and sound, the only light the flickering flames and the occasional flash of lightning from the storm outside.

The world ceased to exist beyond this room, beyond this moment.

Isabella's climax hit her like a wave, a rush of heat and light, her nails digging into Alessio's back as she cried out his name.

The sound, the feel of her around him, sent him over the edge, his release a shuddering, all-consuming force.

They lay entwined, their bodies slick with sweat, the storm outside now a distant murmur. The fire had burned bright and fierce, leaving them both spent, yet somehow more connected than ever.

The Quiet Before the Storm

Morning light filtered through the tattered curtains, casting a soft glow over the room.

Alessio awoke to find Isabella nestled against him, her head resting on his chest, her breathing steady and calm.

He traced the line of her jaw with his finger, marveling at the softness of her skin, the warmth of her body against his.

She stirred, her eyes fluttering open, meeting his gaze with a sleepy smile.

"Good morning," she whispered, her voice husky from sleep.

He smiled, brushing a strand of hair from her face.

"Morning," he replied, his voice rough with emotion he wasn't ready to acknowledge.

They lay there in comfortable silence, the weight of their shared night settling around them.

The world outside was a chaotic mess of alliances, betrayals, and impending war, but in this moment, it was just them—two souls intertwined, seeking solace in each other's arms.

Isabella propped herself up on one elbow, her eyes studying him with an intensity that made him uneasy.

"What happens now?" she asked, her voice tinged with uncertainty.

He sighed, running a hand through his hair. "Now, we face the consequences of our actions. We deal with Marco, with your father, with everyone who stands in our way."

She nodded, her expression hardening with resolve. "And after that?"

"After that," he said, his voice low and serious, "we rebuild. We take what's ours."

She leaned down, pressing a soft kiss to his lips. "Together," she murmured.

"Together," he agreed, pulling her back into his embrace.

But even as they held each other, a nagging feeling gnawed at him—a sense that this peace, this fleeting moment of normalcy, was just the calm before the storm.

And when the storm came, it would tear them apart, body and soul.

He pushed the thought away, focusing instead on the woman in his arms, the woman who had become his partner in every sense of the word. Whatever came next, they would face it together.

But deep down, he knew that some pacts, once made, could never be broken.

And this one—the pact of no return—would change everything.

CHAPTER 19

- Ashes of Loyalty -

THE CITY HUMMED with its usual symphony of distant traffic, murmured conversations, and the occasional blare of a horn. Yet, within the confines of the dimly lit restaurant, a profound silence enveloped Alessio and Marco.

The clinking of silverware and the soft rustling of linen were the only sounds accompanying their tense exchange.

Alessio studied Marco's every movement, every flicker of emotion.

The man before him was a study in contrasts—charming yet duplicitous, confident yet vulnerable. Their shared history was a tapestry woven with threads of camaraderie and rivalry, each encounter adding complexity to their relationship.

"Alessio," Marco began, his voice smooth, betraying no hint of the storm that had raged between them, "it's been too long."

"Indeed," Alessio replied, his tone measured, betraying none of his inner turmoil.

"Time has a way of altering perspectives."

Marco's eyes gleamed with unspoken thoughts. "And yet, some things remain unchanged."

The waiter approached, interrupting the delicate dance of

words. Orders were placed, and the two men sat in an uneasy silence, each contemplating the path that had led them here.

As the meal progressed, their conversation meandered through topics of mutual acquaintances, past exploits, and veiled references to their current standings.

The dance of diplomacy was intricate, each word chosen with precision, each gesture laden with meaning.

Finally, Alessio leaned forward, his gaze unwavering.

"Marco, the Moretti family has always valued strength and loyalty. In these times, alliances are not just beneficial; they are essential."

Marco met his gaze, a flicker of understanding passing between them.

"And what do you propose?"

"A partnership," Alessio stated, his voice firm. "Access to the southern docks, a shared stake in the upcoming shipments, and a unified front against our common adversaries."

Marco's fingers drummed lightly on the table, a sign of contemplation.

"Trust is a luxury, Alessio. One that is earned, not freely given."

Alessio's lips curled into a semblance of a smile. "Then consider this the first installment of our mutual investment."

The agreement was sealed with a handshake, each man acutely aware of the weight it carried.

Yet, beneath the veneer of camaraderie, both knew that this alliance was but a strategic move in a larger game—a game where trust was a currency neither could afford to spend freely.

Silent Codes

The night was a canvas painted with strokes of moonlight and shadow. Within the sanctuary of his study, Alessio sat before an array of glassware, each piece meticulously arranged.

The soft glow of a solitary lamp illuminated his hands as he began the ritual.

The Moretti glass codes—a system of communication passed down through generations—were more than mere reflections; they were lifelines.

Each angle, each refraction held meaning, a language understood only by those initiated.

As his fingers danced over the glass, arranging and rearranging, the patterns began to form. A message materialized: *"LIE TO HIM. TRUST ME."*

Isabella's face appeared in his mind's eye, her features illuminated by the same lamp, her hands moving with practiced ease as she deciphered the code.

Their shared history, their clandestine communications, had always been their tether to reality amidst the chaos.

Moments later, a response flickered back: *"Understood. Proceed with caution."*

Alessio exhaled slowly, the weight of their situation pressing down upon him. Each move was a calculated risk, each decision a potential misstep.

Yet, this was the path they had chosen, and there was no turning back.

The Unforgivable Task

The warehouse was a monolith of steel and shadow, its very presence a testament to the undercurrents of power and secrecy that flowed through the city.

Inside, the air was thick with tension, the faint scent of oil and metal permeating the space.

Alessio stood before Marco, the weight of the task at hand settling heavily upon him.

"Rafael Vega," Marco began, his voice devoid of emotion, "once a trusted member, now a traitor. His actions have endangered us all."

Alessio's gaze remained impassive. "And you want me to eliminate him."

Marco's eyes bore into him.

"His betrayal is a cancer. It must be excised before it spreads."

The photograph was placed before Alessio—a man with haunted eyes, standing amidst shadows. A face that once held camaraderie, now a symbol of treachery.

"Consider it done," Alessio replied, his voice betraying no hint of the turmoil churning within.

The night was an orchestra of sounds—distant traffic, the rustling of leaves, the soft patter of rain.

Alessio moved through the streets with purpose, each step measured, each breath controlled.

Rafael's hideout was a nondescript building, its exterior blending seamlessly with the urban sprawl. Inside, the atmosphere was oppressive, the air thick with the scent of damp and decay.

Rafael knelt before him, his hands bound, his eyes reflecting a mixture of fear and defiance.

"Alessio," he began, his voice trembling, "I never wanted this. They threatened my family. I had no choice."

Alessio's gaze softened imperceptibly. "Choices define us, Rafael. You chose this path."

A silence enveloped them, heavy with unspoken words.

"Please," Rafael pleaded, "spare me. I'll disappear. Start anew.

Just... don't kill me."

Alessio's hand hovered over the gun, the weight of the decision pressing down upon him. The code, the alliance, Isabella's face—all flashed before him.

With a swift motion, he lowered the weapon, signaling to his men. "Let him go," he commanded.

Rafael scrambled to his feet, casting a final, grateful glance before disappearing into the night.

Alessio remained, alone with his thoughts, the echoes of his actions reverberating within him.

The Weight of Loyalty

Loyalty had a cost.

And Alessio Moretti had been paying the debt in blood and silence for years.

He stood at the edge of his office window, looking out over Verona, the city glittering beneath the pale haze of fog and neon.

He knew every corner of it—where bodies had been buried, where deals had been made, where blood had dried on cobblestones like old wine. From this height, it looked clean. Innocent, almost.

But Alessio knew better. The city was just like him—elegant on the surface, rotting underneath.

A quiet knock broke the silence.

It was Matteo, his consigliere, the man who'd been by his side since the night Alessio put a bullet in his own uncle for betrayal.

"The traitor?" Alessio asked, his voice low.

Matteo gave a single nod. "Marco believes he's dead. The body we switched is in place. But it won't hold forever."

Alessio didn't turn around. "It doesn't have to. Just long enough."

There was a pause. Then: "You're sure about this? Letting Rafael live?"

Alessio's silence was answer enough. Matteo didn't press further. He never did.

After the door shut, Alessio walked to the decanter on the sideboard. Poured two fingers of whiskey. Let it burn down his throat like penance.

He had made his choice.

To protect Isabella. To move closer to Marco. To pretend to be loyal to the man who wanted to destroy them both.

And he had lied to everyone—except her.

The irony wasn't lost on him. He'd built his empire on ruthless loyalty.

Made men bleed for less than half the betrayal he was now committing in silence. But he couldn't kill Rafael.

Not just because the man had once saved Alessio's life during a gunfight at the Adriatic border. But because his death would have been for show.

A symbol, nothing more. And Alessio had grown tired of sacrificing good men for bad optics.

He ran a hand through his hair, tension tightening in his jaw.

Everything was shifting now. The war was no longer about borders or shipments. It was personal. Marco had crossed a line the moment he threatened Isabella.

And Alessio was done playing cautious.

He turned toward the desk, picked up the folded note Isabella had slipped into his jacket at the Romano estate two nights ago.

It was simple. Barely a sentence.

"I know what you're doing. Just don't lose yourself in the war."

He traced the edge of the paper with his thumb. She always saw through him. Past the masks, the suits, the violence.

He didn't deserve her.

But he would burn the world for her.

Alessio folded the note and slid it into the back of his wallet. He'd carry it with him until the war ended—or until he did.

His phone buzzed. A secure line. One of their men at the docks.

He answered. "Speak."

"It's done. The Romano shipment was delayed just like you planned. Marco's furious. He's blaming the Russians."

"Good. Let him."

"And, boss… he's asking questions about Isabella."

A silence.

Alessio's voice dropped to a dangerous whisper. "If he touches her—"

"He won't. She's still safe. But he's suspicious."

Alessio ended the call without another word.

Safe wasn't enough anymore. Not with Marco getting desperate.

He turned to his safe, punched in the code, and pulled out a folder labeled *Operazione Sirena*—the final phase of the plan he'd built in shadows.

He had one shot to dismantle Marco Romano from the inside. If it failed, it wouldn't just cost him his empire. It would cost Isabella her life.

And that, he couldn't live with.

He stared down at the blueprints, the surveillance photos, the burner phone logs, the coded ledgers Isabella had stolen and smuggled out in perfume boxes.

They were in too deep now.

One wrong move, and it would all fall apart.

But Alessio wasn't afraid of falling. He'd done it before.

He was afraid of falling alone.

Guilt That Doesn't Wash Off

The Moretti safehouse in the hills was quiet—too quiet.

Alessio stood beneath the shower, the water scalding hot, cascading over muscle and scar.

Steam rose around him like smoke from a burning chapel.

He braced a hand against the marble tile, eyes shut. The blood was gone—scrubbed away from his skin. But it clung to his memory, persistent, sticky.

He saw Rafael's eyes—terrified, grateful. A man who should be dead. A man Marco believed *was* dead.

Alessio had lied to Marco. Had buried another man in Rafael's place. Had let the traitor live.

And he'd done it for a war he still wasn't sure he'd win.

He stepped out of the shower, dried off with the precision of a soldier, and dressed in silence. Charcoal suit. Black tie.

A gun holstered beneath his jacket. The weight was familiar. Comforting.

In the mirror, he adjusted his cufflinks and saw his father's eyes looking back at him. Cold. Unforgiving.

He wondered what his father would say if he were alive.

Would he be proud?

Or would he call Alessio a hypocrite—for preaching loyalty and practicing betrayal?

He walked to the kitchen. Isabella was there, barefoot,

wearing one of his shirts. Her hair was wet. Her eyes were tired.

She looked up as he entered, and for a moment, they didn't speak.

Then, softly, she said, "You didn't kill him."

"No."

"You should have."

"Maybe."

"Why didn't you?"

Alessio looked at her—the woman who had defied her father, risked everything, stepped into the fire for him.

He couldn't lie to her.

"Because I've killed too many men who didn't deserve it. And I'm tired of being a weapon."

Isabella walked toward him slowly. Her hand touched his face.

"And if that makes you weak?"

"Then I'll die weak."

She smiled. Not with her lips, but with her eyes. And it broke him.

Alessio pulled her into his arms and held her there. Not like a man claiming something, but like a man terrified of losing everything.

They stood there, wrapped in silence and scars, two broken people with blood on their hands and ghosts in their beds.

Outside, the wind howled.

Inside, nothing moved. Not even time.

CHAPTER 20

- Wedding Bells -

THE MIRRORS WERE cruel , they reflected the fragile facade of perfection—her porcelain skin, the delicate lace of the gown, the veil that hung like a shroud.

Every inch of her was a lie, sculpted for the wedding that would never be hers.

She felt the weight of the silk pressing down on her chest, choking her with every breath. The gown was white, but her heart was black with rage, a stark contrast to the purity the dress symbolized.

Emilio's commands rang out like a conductor's baton, moving her from fitting to fitting, from dress to dress, as if she were nothing more than an ornament to be displayed.

She held herself stiff, numb against the whispers of the seamstresses and the clink of lace and satin as they adjusted her.

But it was the silence between the movements that felt loudest—the deafening quiet of a woman who had already been promised to someone else, a woman whose heart had been stolen before she could even own it.

Her thoughts turned dark, volatile. Each breath in was a rebellion, a sharp edge against the suffocating calm of her situation.

Her fingers twitched with the desire to rip the veil from her face, to tear the dress from her body and burn it. But she held herself still, because she knew this act of submission wasn't just a public performance—it was survival.

The dress was no longer a symbol of love. It was a chain, a reminder of the life she would never have.

The Gift Box

The note arrived like a warning in a red box—its edges sharp enough to cut if handled too roughly. She didn't open it immediately. Instead, she stared at the box, her mind racing with a thousand thoughts.

The anticipation of its contents gnawed at her insides. A gift. From him.

When she finally untied the crimson ribbon, there was only one item inside: a red veil. Blood red. Almost as if it were dipped in the promise of violence.

She felt her pulse quicken as she read the note attached to it:

"Patience."

The single word felt like a slap, cold and dismissive. It was as if Alessio was mocking her, playing with the strings of her emotions as if they were a puppet's, pulling and tugging at her heart and her will.

But beneath the sting, something else flickered—something dangerous, something that both terrified and excited her.

Patience.

The word echoed in her mind like a curse, like a promise. She had no choice but to wait, to endure. And when the time came, she would make her move.

Because patience wasn't her ally—it was her weapon.

The Trial Dinner

The soft clinking of cutlery filled the air, but in Isabella's ears, it was the sound of chains rattling.

Every movement felt like a slow unraveling, each second she sat at the table with Marco, each word that escaped her lips, was a sacrifice of her very soul.

She had learned long ago how to wear her silence like a second skin, how to hide the chaos inside with the perfect performance.

But tonight? Tonight, the façade felt thinner than ever.

Marco's laugh echoed across the table, his charm polished, his gaze fixed on her as though she were the only thing that mattered. He was proud of her. Proud of his prize.

And yet, she couldn't bring herself to return the affection. There was no warmth in her smile, no genuine sparkle in her eyes.

There was only a cold, calculating gaze that met his, all while she painted herself as the perfect fiancée, the perfect daughter.

"You look stunning, Isabella," Marco's voice broke through her thoughts, a smooth whisper meant only for her.

"You know, I couldn't have asked for a better woman."

A shudder ran through her at the words, the implications so insidious it made her stomach turn. Her eyes flickered over the table, meeting the approving glances of the other guests, the unspoken congratulations hidden behind their painted smiles.

"Thank you," she replied softly, her voice far too sweet, far too compliant.

But under the surface, the venom brewed. She knew the game she was playing.

And she hated it. The rage she had buried so deep, the years of fighting, of refusing to submit to the life laid before her—it all came rushing back now.

A tidal wave of fury that threatened to break free.

When she lifted her glass to toast, her fingers trembled slightly—not from nerves, but from the raw power of the rebellion building in her chest.

Her gaze met Marco's, and she held his stare with a deadly calm, her lips curling into a smile that was anything but kind.

"To the future," he said, raising his glass.

To the future. The words felt like daggers in her ears. They weren't her future. They were his. His future, his plans, his ownership of her. It made her sick to her core.

As she clinked her glass against his, she allowed herself one fleeting moment of rebellion.

Her heart, the dark corner of it she had fought so hard to keep hidden, screamed. *This wasn't her future.* Not anymore.

She took a sip of the wine, its sweetness clashing with the bitterness in her throat. Every drop felt like a contract she never signed, every sip a reminder of the cage she was locked in.

Marco watched her, satisfied in his delusion that he had her.

But her mind was already on fire with thoughts of escape, thoughts of something far darker.

Her thoughts drifted to Alessio. The note. The red veil. *Patience.*

The word burned in her veins, like a slow-moving poison. She had to wait. But every passing second, every minute spent pretending—she could feel herself breaking apart, a small fracture forming deep inside her.

Not yet.

She squeezed her hand around her glass tighter, the crystal pressing into her palm, anchoring her to the moment. It wasn't her time. But it would come. And when it did, Marco would be nothing more than a memory, a chapter she would erase from her story.

As the night dragged on, the warmth of the wine and the company made her feel heavy, suffocated. She could barely hear the conversation around her, the laughter, the polite inquiries.

It was all white noise now. She was far away, lost in the storm that churned inside her.

The evening dragged like an eternity, the same empty smiles exchanged again and again, the same empty promises spoken over the meal that had no taste to her.

She barely noticed when dessert was brought out, the delicate soufflé that sat in front of her, a final symbol of this mockery of a life.

And then the evening reached its bitter end. The guests stood, the laughter continued, but Isabella remained seated at the table, her glass now empty, her thoughts consumed with the one thing that mattered.

The one person who could change everything.

Marco leaned over, his lips brushing her ear. "I'm so glad you're mine," he whispered, his words drenched in ownership.

Mine. The word was a lie. A suffocating lie.

Her stomach twisted, but she held it together, her breath steady, her gaze fixed.

She met his eyes once more, her smile now a perfect, cold imitation of affection.

"To the future, Marco," she said, her voice steady as steel.

And as she rose from the table, her glass held high in a perfect toast, she saw the truth for what it was. She would never be his. Not truly. She would never belong to anyone but herself.

She smiled at Marco and toasted to the future.

But her glass held poison. And her heart, a dagger.

CHAPTER 21

- Red Lace & Ruin -

THE NIGHT PULSED WITH heat, music thumping through the walls of the private venue, a trap dressed in silk and secrets. The bachelorette party was in full swing—laughter, clinking glasses, and the scent of expensive perfume mingling with the humid summer air.

But amid the glitter and the glamour, Isabella's heart beat with a rhythm that had nothing to do with the festivities.

She had felt him the moment he stepped into the shadows.

Alessio was there, just beyond her reach, hidden like a specter in the darkened corners of the room.

His presence was undeniable, a magnetic force pulling at her even though she hadn't yet seen him.

She tried to ignore the sharp tug in her chest—the pull that always came with him.

But the way he moved in the shadows, like a predator waiting, sent a chill through her veins.

Her skin tingled as she moved among the guests, pretending to laugh, pretending to be just another woman in a world where nothing felt real anymore.

But Alessio was a reminder of everything that was.

Everything she could never have.

And yet, everything she would destroy to make her own.

When she slipped into the wine cellar later, alone and hidden beneath a mask of smiles, she hadn't expected him to follow. But the doors creaked open, and there he stood, like an omen, his presence a threat that was both comforting and dangerous.

His eyes locked on hers, a silent acknowledgment that neither of them were playing by the rules.

Before she could speak, his hand was on her wrist, pulling her toward him. There was no hesitation, no words needed. It was instinct—raw, desperate. The scent of aged wine and dust hung in the air as his lips brushed her ear.

"I thought you might need a reminder of what you're fighting for," Alessio's voice was a low rasp, full of danger.

She looked up at him, eyes wide, heart racing. "I don't need anything from you."

His thumb ran over her pulse, a dangerous smile curling at the corner of his lips.

"You don't have to admit it, Isabella. But you know you need this."

For one agonizing second, she considered throwing herself into his arms, giving into the madness.

But the reality of the game she was playing came crashing back—the stakes were too high, the risk too great.

With a hard, final look, she pushed him away, stepping back. "Not tonight."

Alessio didn't argue, but his gaze never wavered, and for a moment, it felt like he was stripping her bare with just his eyes.

She had to leave.

The Seduction Plan

The hours that followed were a blur of strategy and careful moves. The wine cellar had only served to ignite something deeper, darker inside her.

Alessio's words echoed in her mind. *You know you need this.*

But what was "this"? Was it power? Control? Or simply the desperate hunger that consumed them both?

The answer was unclear. But one thing was certain—there was only one way to win this game, and it wasn't by following the rules.

The plan was simple. Marco's guard was always tight. But even the most well-guarded fortress could be breached if you were patient, if you moved carefully enough.

Marco trusted her. He saw only the obedient fiancée—the woman who existed to please him, to belong to him. But beneath that mask, beneath the silk and lace, there was something else. Something that could unravel him.

Isabella's fingers brushed over the red lace in her hands. The dress she had worn earlier—the one Marco adored—had served its purpose. But now, it was time to make the final move.

Alessio had come to her in the shadows for a reason. And now, he would be the one to watch. She would use Marco's desire to bring him closer, to let down his guard in the most dangerous of ways.

One Night, One Lie

Marco was waiting for her when she returned. His arms were open, the smile on his face too wide, too insistent.

This was the game now. She had to play her part, had to make him believe that she belonged to him.

But every inch of her was calculating, every movement measured.

Isabella stepped into the room slowly, her lips curling into a perfect, obedient smile.

"I'm yours, Marco," she said softly, the words as poisonous as the venom she would soon unleash.

His eyes gleamed, pleased with the affirmation, with the control he thought he had over her. But she knew better. She knew exactly what she was doing, how she was twisting everything they had into something unrecognizable.

As Marco moved toward her, she didn't flinch. She didn't pull away. She didn't even let herself feel the revulsion that clawed at her insides.

Instead, she let him believe he had her, all while keeping her mind focused on the one thing that mattered—*Alessio*.

The room was warm, the lights dimmed low, but every breath she took was a reminder of the game they were all playing.

And with every touch Marco placed on her body, every whispered word, Isabella counted the heartbeats.

One for Alessio. One for war.

And when Marco moved to kiss her, when his hands reached for the buttons of her dress, she froze him with a touch.

"No," she whispered, eyes dark with something far more dangerous.

"You don't touch me. You never will."

But Marco didn't know that yet. He only knew that she had already made him believe she was his.

It was a twisted, deadly dance. As Marco positioned her, his hands on her hips, Isabella didn't let him touch her the way he wanted.

She straddled him, a slow, calculated move to make him believe he had all the control.

Her mind spun, counting the beats in her chest, each one a

painful reminder of the cost of her game. One for Alessio.

One for war. One for the destruction that was coming for all of them.

The tension between them was thick, a knot that had yet to unravel. Marco's breath hitched, his hands grasping her waist, desperate. He thought he had her. He thought she was his.

But Isabella didn't feel the same. She didn't let him have what he wanted, not fully. She let him believe she was lost in him, that she was willingly his.

But she wasn't.

Not anymore.

Every second, every movement, was a calculated step closer to the storm that would shatter everything. She was playing a game with no rules, and the stakes were higher than anyone realized.

Isabella's heart thudded in her chest, louder than it had ever been. Every moment she spent in Marco's arms felt like a betrayal.

But it wasn't just Marco she was betraying—it was herself.

She was losing herself piece by piece in this war, and she couldn't stop it.

Not until she had what she wanted. Not until she had Alessio. Not until the final blow was struck.

But as she pulled away from Marco, the thrill of manipulation lingering in her veins, she couldn't escape the hollow feeling in her chest. The game was far from over, but a part of her felt like she was already dying.

Alessio didn't know where she was that night.
Only that she didn't call and that nearly broke him.

CHAPTER 22

- The Heir of Secrets -

ALESSIO LEANED OVER his desk, eyes fixed on the flash drive in front of him. It was small, inconspicuous, but it was the key to everything—the one piece of the puzzle he hadn't been able to crack.

The drive was a whisper from the past, a shadow buried beneath years of secrets and lies, and it had only arrived at his hands through the most dangerous of methods.

His hacker, a wiry genius with more tattoos than a man should have, had managed to recover it from the ruins of the Romano network.

They'd told him the Romano family had burned everything they could, but this drive… this was something they hadn't accounted for. It was too dangerous to let go.

Alessio plugged it into his laptop, the familiar hum of the machine filling the silence of his office.

He didn't need to see the files; he could feel the weight of them, the tension hanging in the air, like the moment before an explosion.

The screen flickered as the files loaded, and Alessio's fingers hovered over the keyboard, waiting.

His breath stilled as the first document appeared—a ledger.

The Romano family's dirty laundry laid bare. Names. Dates. Places.

All carefully documented, each entry a potential weapon, each name a future target.

His eyes scanned the list quickly, his pulse steady, his focus absolute. But then he froze, his heart missing a beat.

There it was. Paolo Moretti's name, neatly tucked under a list of payments and illegal transactions. It wasn't just a name—there was a description beside it: *traitor*.

His uncle.

The word burned in his throat, choking him. He stared at the screen, unable to look away, as if somehow, if he didn't blink, the words would change, would disappear.

Paolo was a traitor? To his family? To *him*?

It didn't make sense. Or maybe it made too much sense. His uncle, the one who had always been the voice of reason, the calm in the storm, the man who had groomed him to take control of the family.

How could he betray them all?

Alessio's fingers clenched, and his knuckles went white. His breath was shallow, his mind racing. He needed to know more, needed to understand how deep the betrayal went.

But there was no more time to process it—he had to act. Now. He downloaded the file, but even as the progress bar slowly filled, he already knew one thing for certain.

This was a war that could never be fought with honor. And he had no intention of losing it.

The Archive Room

The archive room was buried deep beneath the Moretti estate —accessible only through a labyrinth of hallways that wound like a snake through the mansion's bowels. Few had ever seen the room.

Fewer still knew what lay hidden within it.

Alessio stood in the doorway, the stale air of the room hitting him like a wave. The thick scent of old paper, dust, and forgotten history filled his lungs as he stepped inside.

Rows of shelves lined the walls, filled with books, files, and photographs—records of a legacy that had been carefully constructed and then hidden away.

His father's office had been the center of the family's power, but it was here, in this forgotten corner, that secrets festered.

His eyes scanned the shelves, his mind already calculating the steps to find what he needed. It was there, tucked behind a row of dusty files, that he found a box—small, weathered, a relic of a time long past.

Inside was a single letter, wrapped in thick, yellowed paper. No address. No name. Only a seal in dark red wax—his father's seal.

Alessio's hands trembled as he carefully broke the seal, unrolling the letter.

His father's handwriting, sharp and precise, stared back at him.

"If you're reading this, they already betrayed you."

The words froze him. His father had known. Had known that the treachery ran deep, that the family was fractured before his death.

That the trust he had placed in Paolo had been a mistake all along.

There were no comforting words here, no answers, only a simple, brutal truth.

"They will come for you next. Trust no one. Not even your own blood."

The letter felt like a weight in his chest, its presence suffocating. His father had known what was coming—and had prepared him for it, even if he couldn't have foreseen the full extent of the betrayal.

Alessio stood still for a moment, the letter still in his hands, as the silence of the room pressed in on him. He'd been raised to believe that family meant everything.

That loyalty was a bond forged in blood. But this—this was a new kind of war. One where no one was safe.

He stuffed the letter into his coat pocket, the ink still burning in his mind. There was no going back now. The walls were closing in, and every step he took forward only led him deeper into the darkness.

The Rage

Alessio's mind was a storm. He stormed out of the archive room, the words from his father still fresh in his mind. *Trust no one.*

His breath was ragged as he made his way through the mansion, his steps echoing down the empty hallways. His body was a coil of tension, his thoughts a maelstrom of fury.

Every step was a countdown. He had to confront Paolo. He had to know if his uncle was the one behind it all.

The door to Paolo's study was slightly ajar. The lights inside were dim, but the shadows clung to the edges of the room, casting long, ominous shapes on the walls.

Alessio stepped inside, his eyes already searching for him.

Paolo was sitting at his desk, his back turned, a glass of whiskey in his hand. He didn't turn around as Alessio entered, but his smile was evident in the tilt of his head, the casual arrogance in his posture.

"You've been busy, Alessio," Paolo said, his voice smooth and patronizing.

Alessio's fingers clenched into fists at his sides. "What do you know about the Romano ledger?"

Paolo chuckled, a dark, amused sound.

"I know you've been digging in places you shouldn't. I warned you about that."

"I'm done with the lies," Alessio hissed, stepping closer, his voice sharp as a blade.

"Tell me the truth. Were you the one who sold us out?"

Paolo finally turned in his chair, his eyes cold and calculating.

"You think I'm the traitor?" he asked, a smirk playing on his lips.

"You've always been too eager to blame others, Alessio. But I suppose that's what happens when you don't have a real family to turn to."

Alessio's temper flared, his hands twitching as he fought the urge to strike. But he kept his voice steady, a dangerous calm that made the tension in the room palpable.

"Tell me what you know. Now."

Paolo leaned back in his chair, as if enjoying this moment of control.

"Your mother wasn't an accident, Alessio. Do you really think I didn't know what happened that night?" His voice was dark, almost conspiratorial.

"She died because she had to. The family couldn't afford her weakness. She wasn't strong enough for this world."

The words hit Alessio like a punch to the gut, his chest tightening, his vision blurring.

His mother. *Not an accident?*

The anger that boiled inside him was something primal, something he had never fully understood until now. The betrayal wasn't just about business. It was about family—his blood, his legacy. And his uncle had a hand in it all.

Without thinking, Alessio moved. The desk slammed against the wall as he grabbed Paolo by the throat, lifting him off the chair.

Paolo's eyes widened, but the smirk never left his face.

"You don't know anything about loyalty, do you?" Alessio spat.

Paolo's hand gripped his wrist, but his voice was calm, even amused.

"You'll kill me? Do you really think that will make everything better, Alessio?"

The words were like poison, making everything sharper, more dangerous. Alessio's heart was pounding in his chest, his vision narrowing.

He didn't know who to kill first—the man who had destroyed his family, or the truth that would tear everything apart.

Alessio didn't know who to kill first—his uncle, or the truth.

CHAPTER 23

- A Rose for the Dead -

THEY BURIED MATTEO in the garden of saints, beneath a marble angel with its face turned away—like even heaven was ashamed of what had happened.

The skies held their breath as Isabella Romano stepped out of the car, her heels slicing through the wet gravel like declarations.

She wore no veil. No tear-stained mascara. Just a black dress, severe and spotless, and eyes that hadn't blinked since they told her it was suicide.

Matteo had been the youngest of them. Twenty-four. Bright-eyed, arrogant, and stupid enough to believe the family wouldn't turn on its own. A cousin. A shadow of her childhood.

They'd played hide-and-seek in the villa hallways before either of them knew how sharp a secret could be.

Now he was in a coffin. Polished oak. Shut tight like the lies that placed him there.

"They said he left a note," her aunt whispered to no one in particular. "That he felt… cornered."

Isabella stared at the casket. She didn't believe in cornered men killing themselves. Not in this world. Not in this family. She believed in bullets behind the ear, wrists slit and staged with care, windows opened wide to mimic the fall.

Her eyes drifted to Caterina—Matteo's sister—who stood statue-still beside the grave, her hands clenched so tightly her nails dug into skin.

Blood was blooming in her palms. But she didn't cry. She didn't scream.

And that silence said everything.

It was murder. Political. Cold. And everyone in attendance knew it. They just kept their heads bowed like sheep with designer sunglasses and whispered condolences like lullabies to guilt.

Isabella said nothing. Grief had no language here. Only calculations.

Her grandfather stood near the altar, ringed by soldiers in fine suits, rosaries wrapped like snakes around their fists. Emilio didn't look at Matteo's casket once.

Not even when the priest spoke the boy's name. Power didn't mourn. It moved on.

And Isabella?

She mourned, yes—but not just for Matteo.

She mourned the death of the illusion that her bloodline could ever be redeemed.

Her Breaking Point

They lowered the coffin. Dirt struck the wood with soft, brutal thuds. The sound echoed in her bones.

Isabella stood until the last flower was thrown. Until the last lie was spoken. Until the last pair of polished shoes turned away from grief like it was contagious.

Then she walked. Alone.

She didn't take the car back to the villa. She walked along the winding, empty roads of Palermo's outskirts, heels discarded, bare feet cutting on gravel.

The hem of her black dress clung to her calves as if even the fabric didn't want to let her go. And still, she kept walking.

Until the gates appeared.

Campo delle Ombre.
The cemetery where the old Romanos slept. Where secrets were buried in neat rows beside saints and sinners alike. Matteo didn't belong here.

He belonged in light, in the reckless kind of youth that still believed in mercy.

But now his name was etched in cold stone like every other sacrifice made to keep power alive.

She stopped in front of his grave. The freshly turned soil was still damp, uneven. A white rose had been placed gently on top. She stared at it.

Then pulled a single black rose from her coat pocket.

She'd brought it herself.

She didn't cry. She pressed the rose into the dirt, her fingers trembling—not from grief, but from rage laced with finality. The kind that settles like steel behind the ribs.

"I'll remember what they did to you," she whispered, voice raw.

Her cousin's voice echoed in her memory—Matteo at sixteen, cocky and laughing, calling her principessa. Swearing he'd make something of himself without needing to kiss the ring.

The last time they spoke, he told her to be careful.

That Emilio was grooming Marco to be more than heir—he was teaching him how to kill with politics and smiles.

Now Matteo was dead.

Isabella didn't break down. She broke open.

Because it hit her with unshakable clarity: this would never stop. Not with Matteo. Not with the others. Not with her.

Her family would kill for power.

And she'd be next if she stopped pretending.

So she stood there, wind catching the hem of her dress, and for the first time since the engagement announcement, her mask slipped. Not into despair.

Into war.

Her voice was steady when she said it aloud to the marble cross behind her cousin's name:

"They won't bury me alive. Not without a fight."

Back to Alessio

The city blurred past her in streaks of gold and ash as the car sped through narrow streets. Isabella didn't remember getting in.

She didn't remember telling the driver where to go.

Only that her hands were shaking and her mouth tasted like grave dirt.

She didn't stop to knock when she reached Alessio's apartment.

She pushed the door open like a storm and found him shirtless, sitting on the edge of the bed, a gun dismantled in his lap and war behind his eyes.

He rose the second he saw her.

"Isa—"

"Don't speak."

Her voice was ragged. Ruined. Her pupils dilated like she couldn't tell if she was prey or predator anymore. Rain clung to her hair, her lashes, her neckline.

The silk of her dress was soaked and clung to her skin like a second betrayal.

"I need to forget," she said.

There was no seduction in it. Just demand. Just grief. Just need, sharp and splintered.

Alessio's jaw clenched. He stepped forward. "Are you hurt?"

"Yes," she said. "But not where you can see."

She didn't want tenderness.

She wanted to be broken open, piece by piece, until grief had no place to hide inside her body. Until all that remained was skin, breath, and heat.

So she kissed him like she was starving for violence and he answered like a sinner dragged to the altar.

He slammed her against the wall. Her legs wrapped around his waist. Their mouths collided, brutal and punishing. His fingers dug into her thighs. Hers clawed at his back.

There was no patience. No poetry. Just *desperation.*

He tore her dress down the middle, silk ripping like a scream.

"Tell me to stop," he growled, breath hot against her throat.

"I'll kill you if you do," she gasped.

He carried her to the bed, dropped her onto the mattress like she weighed less than the sins they carried, and ruined her slowly, with unrelenting hands and teeth. There were no soft words. Only harsh breaths and the crash of flesh against sheets.

Pain drove it. Fury shaped it. Love had no room here.

And still, somewhere in the way she arched into him—like she'd been waiting her whole life to fall apart in his arms—something tender cracked beneath the violence.

When it was over, they were tangled and trembling.

She buried her face in his chest.

And said nothing.

Because there were no words for what she'd just given him.

And none for what he'd taken without even asking.

CHAPTER 24

- The Serpent's Bite -

THE FILE WAS old , yellowed edges, timestamped photos, faded bloodstains beneath typed names.

She shouldn't have opened it.

The manila folder had been buried inside a false drawer in her father's study. She found it by accident—except nothing felt accidental anymore.

Her hands trembled as she turned the page.

Photo: Alessio's mother.
Cause of death: Car bomb.
Signed: Emilio Romano.
Target: Luciana Moretti.
Justification: Asset elimination. Collateral: Acceptable.

Her breath left her in a stagger.

"No," she whispered. "No, no…"

Emilio's script was clean. Precise. Her father's name signed like a death sentence.

The next page made her knees buckle.

CONFIRMATION: Paolo Moretti alerted the Moretti heir. Subject refused to cooperate. Surveillance ceased.

Paolo hadn't betrayed the Morettis.

He tried to protect Luciana.

He tried—and failed.

And now Alessio was hunting Paolo for a crime her father committed.

She clutched the pages to her chest like they could shield her from the avalanche roaring in her mind.

Rage, grief, dread—they braided inside her ribs like thorns, tightening until she couldn't breathe.

Alessio had to know.

But when she looked up from the pages, she realized something too late:

The house was too quiet.

And her father's watch was missing from the desk.

The mansion loomed before him like the kingdom of a snake. Windows lit like eyes. Shadows slithering beneath chandeliers.

He didn't knock.

He walked in with a gun and the weight of twenty years of vengeance burning under his skin.

Marco tried to intercept him at the stairwell.

Alessio shoved the man into a marble pillar so hard the crack echoed like bone.

"Where's Paolo?" he growled.

Emilio emerged from the hallway like a specter already expecting blood.

"Looking for ghosts?" he asked calmly. "Your father used to do the same before he lost his mind."

"Don't talk about my father," Alessio said, voice sharp as broken glass.

Then Isabella appeared.

Her face was pale. Her eyes, wet with secrets. She held the folder in her hands like it weighed more than the gun at Alessio's side.

"Stop," she breathed. "It's not Paolo. It was—"

Too late.

A door creaked.

Behind him: Paolo, bruised but standing. Holding no weapon. Only war in his eyes.

"You don't want to do this, *figlio mio*," Paolo said.

Alessio raised his gun.

"I should've pulled the trigger years ago."

And then—

"*Enough!*" Emilio shouted, stepping between them.

His hand moved like a blur.

And suddenly, his gun was aimed at Alessio.

Gun to Her Head

The air in the Romano study thickened—choked by gunpowder ghosts and promises that had long since turned to poison.

Alessio's eyes burned red. Not with rage anymore. With betrayal.

His gun was steady, pointed at Paolo's chest. And Paolo, older but unflinching, stared back at the boy he once helped raise. The boy now ready to pull the trigger.

"Do it," Paolo said, voice graveled by time and guilt.

"But know this—if you shoot me, you kill the only man who ever tried to protect her."

Alessio hesitated. Just slightly. Enough.

Because that's when he heard it—*the click.*

Not from his own weapon.

From behind him.

"I wouldn't," came Emilio's voice, smooth and venom-laced, like silk dragged across broken glass.

Alessio didn't turn. He didn't need to. He felt the gun pointed between his shoulder blades like a cold brand against his spine.

Isabella's scream tore through the room.

"No!"

She rushed forward, eyes wide, heart ripping through her ribs, but Emilio caught her arm mid-sprint. Spun her toward him.

His other hand—the one holding the pistol—jerked toward her now.

"Stop!" Alessio growled, stepping forward.

The gun redirected instantly—*to her head.*

"Don't test me, boy," Emilio hissed, gripping Isabella with a force that turned her face white. "One wrong move, and I paint these walls with her brains."

Her pulse screamed in her throat. Cold metal pressed against her temple. She didn't cry.

Not this time.

"I trusted you," she whispered, the words for Emilio, but meant for every lie she had ever swallowed like communion.

"You made me your weapon."

Emilio's grip only tightened.

"And you played the role *beautifully,* my little pawn."

Alessio saw red. Not just anger. The kind of red that came before blood. Before death. The kind that meant *there would be no way back.*

"You used her?" he spat, voice cracking like a whip. "You planned this from the start."

Emilio's smirk deepened. "I planned *everything.* Including what happens next."

Boom.

The shot rang out. A single explosion in a room too full of secrets to hold it.

Time broke into fragments.

A gasp. A thud.

The sound of glass shattering—though no window had broken.

Isabella's knees gave out first. Her hands trembled as she reached toward the smoke hanging in the air like a curse.

Her father was still standing.

The gun still warm in his hand.

But Alessio—Alessio was not.

He collapsed in silence, like a prayer left unfinished.

Isabella stared at the blood pooling at her feet.
Her father was still standing. Alessio was not.

CHAPTER 25

- The Wake of a Bullet -

THE ECHO OF THE gunshot still lingered in her ears, even as the night wrapped its cold fingers around the room. The silence that followed was deafening, like the world had paused for a single breath.

But the blood didn't. It slipped from Alessio's body, a slow, steady stream, soaking the marble beneath him in dark, spreading crimson.

Blood had a sound. A soft, wet drip that punctuated the horror in her chest.

Isabella knelt beside him, hands shaking as they hovered over the wound.

She didn't know where to touch, where to press, how to hold the pieces of him together when she was already falling apart herself.

The bullet hadn't killed him—*not yet.* But it had come close. Too close. His breathing was ragged, shallow, each inhale a broken rasp that made her want to scream.

Alessio's eyes fluttered, struggling to stay open, his fingers twitching weakly as if reaching for something—*someone.*

She had to act.

Her hands pressed against the wound, sticky warmth coating her fingers.

"Stay with me," she whispered, her voice cracking. "Stay with me, Alessio, please…"

The Escape

Emilio had fled.

The sound of sirens grew louder in the distance, but they didn't come for her father. They wouldn't. The police—*his police*—would sweep through the mansion, taking the bodies and covering the tracks, just like they had for years.

There would be no justice tonight.

Not for Alessio. Not for the truth that had been buried in the marble halls of her family's empire.

But she couldn't think about that now.

All that mattered was getting him out. Getting him *alive.*

With trembling hands, she pulled out her phone, dialing a number she knew by heart.

The call connected after only one ring.

"Help me," she whispered, her voice barely audible over the thundering in her chest.

"I need a safehouse… now."

The voice on the other end didn't ask questions. There was no time for explanations.

The Safehouse

The safehouse was nothing more than an abandoned, crumbling building on the outskirts of the city.

The air inside was thick with dust and mildew, the kind of place where forgotten things go to die. But it was safe—at least for now.

She dragged Alessio through the narrow doorway, half carrying him, half pleading with the universe to give her the strength to hold him up.

His body was heavy, muscles limp from blood loss, but his heart still beat. Faint. Fading. But it was there.

The mattress on the floor was filthy, but it was the best she could do. She lowered him down as gently as she could, her breath hitching in her throat as his body hit the mattress with a dull thud.

The sound tore through her like the breaking of something fragile, something irreplaceable.

Isabella stood over him, hands stained with his blood, unsure of what to do next.

She had learned many things in the life of a Romano—how to kill, how to lie, how to betray—but not how to heal.

She couldn't save him. *God,* she couldn't even save herself.

But she would try.

Her fingers worked with an urgency that belied her fear, tearing through fabric, cleaning the wound as best as she could with the meager supplies she had scavenged from the first aid kit left behind by whoever used this place before.

She worked in silence, the only sounds in the room the faint dripping of water from the pipes and Alessio's ragged breaths.

He stirred once, his eyes flickering open for the briefest moment, locking onto hers with a look that she couldn't decipher—pain, anger, confusion… trust?

No, not trust.

Trust was a luxury they could no longer afford.

Confession

It took hours for the bleeding to slow, for his breathing to stabilize into something less agonizing. He was alive—barely.

But in the quiet of the night, with the city so far behind them, there was nothing left to do but wait.

And with the waiting came the reckoning.

Isabella sat beside him on the edge of the bed, knees pulled to her chest, watching the slow rise and fall of his chest.

Every breath he took was a reminder of how close she had come to losing him. How close she still was.

Her throat tightened. There were things she hadn't told him.

Things she couldn't say. And yet, in the stillness, with only the sound of his shallow breaths between them, the weight of her secrets became unbearable.

"I never wanted this," she whispered, more to herself than to him. Her voice was a fragile thing, breaking on the edges of her guilt.

"I never wanted any of this."

Alessio didn't respond. He couldn't. His eyes remained closed, his face pale, lips chapped from dehydration. But she kept talking, her words tumbling out in a flood she could no longer control.

"I didn't know," she said, her voice shaking. "About your mother. About Paolo. Emilio... he used me. I was the bait."

Her chest tightened, a sob threatening to tear its way out. She swallowed it down.

"I didn't know. I swear I didn't know."

But that wasn't entirely true.

Because hadn't she always known what her father was capable of? Hadn't she always known that in their world, betrayal was as common as breathing?

She wiped at her eyes with the back of her hand, smearing blood and tears across her cheek.

"You should hate me," she whispered. "You should…"

Through the fog of pain, Alessio stirred.

He didn't move at first. Didn't speak. His body felt like lead, every muscle screaming in protest, his head spinning from the loss of blood.

But he heard her voice. Low, broken. Weaving through his consciousness like a half-remembered dream.

She was crying.

He had never heard her cry before.

And somehow, it was that sound—not the pain in his side, not the sting of the bullet—that hurt the most.

His hand twitched, reaching out to her, brushing against her leg with the barest touch. Her breath hitched. He felt her body go still, her tears pausing for a brief, suspended moment.

"Alessio," she whispered, the word barely a breath.

He forced his eyes open, the dim light of the room blurring as it met his vision.

He blinked, focusing on her. Her face was streaked with blood and tears, her eyes wide and wet, staring down at him like he was something she couldn't bear to lose.

He wasn't used to being looked at like that.

"Don't," he rasped, his voice rough, barely there. "Don't cry."

Her lip trembled, but she pressed it tightly between her teeth, nodding as if she could force herself into silence by sheer will.

"I'm sorry," she whispered, her voice breaking. "I'm so sorry."

He didn't know what she was apologizing for. Maybe for all of it. Maybe for nothing. But in that moment, it didn't matter.

Because she was here. She had chosen to stay.

She didn't know how to save him.
Only that if he died hating her… she wouldn't survive it.

CHAPTER 26

- Venom in the Vows -

PAIN SHARPENS memory, it strips away lies until all you have left... is truth.

Pain had become his closest confidant.

It stalked him from the moment he opened his eyes in that dust-choked safehouse to the hour he returned—wounded but walking—into the lion's den that bore his name.

Pain had a way of burning the falsehoods away. The excuses. The softness.

Alessio had left something behind in that room with Isabella. Something he wasn't sure he'd ever get back.

But he couldn't afford softness anymore. Not now. Not when war was licking at his doorstep.

He stepped back into the villa wearing blood like cologne and silence like armor.

The men who watched him didn't know whether to salute or fear him—and that's exactly how it should be.

Word had traveled fast.

The boss had been shot. The Romano girl had disappeared. Emilio had vanished like smoke in the wind. And Alessio Moretti had crawled out of the fire still breathing, though his eyes said otherwise.

The first thing he did was lock the gates.

The second was call a meeting.

"We're going to war," he said, voice flat as steel. "But first, we play dead."

His men exchanged wary glances, but no one questioned him. Not after the look in his eyes—sharp, unreadable, the look of a man who had died and come back colder.

Alessio Moretti wasn't a man now.

He was a weapon.

The Informant

It took only two days for his network of spies and loyalists to start feeding him intel. Names, faces, bribes that changed hands.

But one report made him stop cold.

A file slid across his desk, and with it, the whisper that tightened his jaw and knotted his gut.

Marco Romano. Emilio Romano. And Isabella.

A *wedding.*

A secret engagement ceremony. No press. No family outside of the two families that mattered. A merging of bloodlines. Power. Territory.

A cage.

She hadn't told him. Not in that safehouse. Not when she sat beside his broken body, whispering truths in a shaking voice. She'd told him everything except *this.*

Unless she didn't know.

Unless…

The file crumpled in his grip.

It was a move meant to provoke. Designed with surgical cruelty.

Emilio's plan was as clear as blood on white silk.

Marry her off while Alessio was still healing. Make her a symbol of unity. Strip her of choice. Use her name as the noose that pulled both families together.

She was the perfect sacrifice.

And Marco—the dutiful son—was nothing more than a placeholder groom. Obedient. Predictable. Forgettable.

Alessio leaned back in his chair, fingers steepled under his chin as he stared out the window.

So this was it. The endgame.

No.

He wouldn't let it end that way. Not while he was still breathing.

He didn't care if Isabella had agreed. He didn't care if she had signed the papers with her own trembling hand.

She was his.

Not in the way men owned women—not in the way Emilio believed—but in the way scars claim skin. In the way trauma binds souls.

And if they tried to tie her to another man in the name of blood and empire?

He'd break their bones with his bare hands.

Strategy in Silence

Alessio spent the next seventy-two hours pretending to be the man they expected him to be.

He sat at the head of the Moretti table. Gave the illusion of control. Held court with capos and advisors who wondered why his eyes looked more dead than alive.

He told them lies.

That he was done chasing ghosts.

That he was willing to discuss terms.

That he would attend the ceremony as a show of peace.

And in the dead of night, when the house slept, he made calls no one could trace. To men in dark cars. To assassins who didn't need names.

To mercenaries who worked for blood and nothing else.

He planned the impossible.

Sabotage the ceremony.

Burn the guest list.

Make the chapel bleed.

And all the while, a single question haunted him:

Did she know?

Was she a pawn again, pushed onto a board designed by men? Or had she willingly stepped back into the cage she'd once tried to escape?

He wasn't ready when the photo arrived.

A courier. Anonymous. No note.

Just an envelope placed in his hand, still warm from the sun.

He opened it without thinking. What stared back at him punched the breath from his chest.

Isabella.

In a white dress.

Not a wedding gown. But close enough. Soft. Feminine. Hollow-eyed. She stood in front of an altar, back straight, expression unreadable. A rehearsal.

A mockery of choice.

He didn't notice the glass shattering in his hand until blood ran down his wrist.

"Burn it," he said to no one.

And someone did.

The Fury Beneath

The night before the engagement ceremony, Alessio stood alone in his old bedroom, the one untouched by time, the one where he had once imagined a different life.

One with her in it.

One where the war ended in peace, not in flames.

But that version of him had died.

He stared at his reflection in the mirror. The scar along his jaw. The hollow beneath his cheekbones. The monster his father had bred and fate had perfected.

There was no wedding tomorrow.

There was a funeral.

Whether it was Marco's or Emilio's, or his own, he didn't care.

Because if Isabella stood beside another man, if she whispered "I do" to anyone but him, if they dared to claim her for their own…

If she said "I do"… he'd burn the chapel to the ground.

CHAPTER 27

- Something Borrowed -

ISABELLA STOOD STILL, a statue draped in ivory. The wedding gown clung to her like a lie sewn in silk. Lace coiled around her arms, delicate and suffocating, as if even the dress knew it was part of a farce.

The veil trembled slightly where it fell, kissed by the tremor in her hands.

Her face in the mirror was the picture of Roman virtue—composed, serene, perfect. But her eyes betrayed her. They were the eyes of a storm.

Behind her, women flitted in and out like shadows—dressing maids, cousins, distant relatives offering compliments that felt like knives. One commented on how lucky she was.

Another whispered that Marco was a powerful man. Isabella only smiled, the way one might at their own execution.

She reached for her lipstick—deep red, like dried blood—and painted her lips without blinking.

Today, she'd play the part. The obedient daughter. The willing bride. The pawn.

But pawns could be sacrificed. Or they could turn the game.

The hall was drenched in excess. Marble floors, gilded

columns, chandeliers that shimmered like glass galaxies overhead. Nobility and crime brushed shoulders here. Judges, dons, bishops. The entire underworld had been invited, dressed to bless a union that was never meant to last.

Marco Romano stood tall beneath the altar's arch, tailored to perfection, smug with power. He scanned the aisle with shark eyes—calculating, possessive.

He didn't smile when he saw Isabella, only nodded, as if approving a weapon newly forged.

She walked toward him on silent feet, not to be given away but to deliver judgment.

The priest spoke. Words blurred.

Isabella didn't hear them. All she heard was her pulse. She glanced at Emilio in the front pew, her father's cold expression barely hiding his anticipation.

He thought he had won. He thought she was caged.

The moment came. "Do you, Isabella Romano..."

She turned to Marco.

The room held its breath.

She kissed him.

It was slow. Almost sensual. She curled her arms around his neck like any docile bride.

And then—

The blade slipped from her sleeve into her hand.

And plunged into his side.

His gasp was swallowed by her lips.

Blood bloomed between them like a red flower, soaking into white silk. Marco staggered, eyes wide with betrayal as he dropped to his knees. Screams erupted.

The priest dropped his Bible.

Emilio rose. Too slow.

Pandemonium.

Gunfire in Gold

The ceremony imploded. Screams ricocheted off marble walls. Some guests fled, others ducked. The pews became shields.

And then, as if summoned by vengeance itself, the doors of the cathedral burst open.

Alessio Moretti walked in through the smoke of chaos like war in human form.

His black suit was streaked with blood from the last skirmish. He looked like a fallen angel—lethal, beautiful, merciless.

He saw her.

And she saw him.

He raised his gun. One shot. A Romano guard collapsed behind her. Another. Blood sprayed against the altar.

And then there was no time.

Gunfire erupted from every corner. Guards. Family. Allies. Enemies. The church became a battlefield.

Isabella crouched behind the altar as bullets carved through sacred wood. She ripped off her heels and pulled the second blade from her garter.

Her dress tore at the thigh. Let them see. Let them bleed.

She sprinted to cover, slicing through a man who raised his pistol too slow. Blood sprayed her veil.

Alessio met her near the altar.

"You stabbed him?" he asked, breathless.

She nodded. "It was the only part of the vows I meant."

They fought side by side—back to back, like predators cornered but not afraid.

The Serpent's Fall

Emilio, slick in his silver tie, tried to flee through the vestry. Isabella saw him.

She followed, heart pounding like war drums. He turned, gun drawn.

But Alessio was already there.

Father. Killer. Liar.

"You used her," Alessio growled. "You made her the bait."

Emilio sneered. "She was always meant to be used."

Alessio lunged.

Gunfire tore through the room. A bullet grazed Emilio's arm. Another shattered a statue. Emilio ducked and fired wildly.

One shot hit Alessio—shoulder, tearing flesh.

He fell.

Isabella screamed, running to him, hands slipping over blood.

Emilio fled as sirens wailed in the distance. Corrupt officers would cover his trail.

But Isabella didn't care.

Alessio was breathing. Barely.

She cradled him, dress soaked in crimson.

The aftermath was ash and broken pews.

Marco writhed on the floor, groaning, barely conscious. The wedding cake lay splattered in a corner, soaked in someone's blood.

Guests who hadn't fled were arrested—or executed by guards who no longer knew which side they served.

But none of it mattered.

Isabella pulled Alessio to his feet, shoulder bleeding, eyes heavy with pain.

They vanished into the smoke together, fugitives of love and war.

Blood smeared her veil. Her hands. Her mouth.
She kissed Alessio anyway. Like she belonged to the war.

CHAPTER 28

- The Devil's Confession -

THE TRUTH WAS never meant to come to light. That's why he buried it in bodies and burned the rest.

They dragged Emilio Romano into the Moretti estate in chains. Not the gold ones he preferred. These were iron, rusting, biting into flesh with every jostled step. The guards didn't speak. Neither did he.

Alessio stood at the end of the corridor like a shadow waiting to swallow him whole. Blood still stained his shirt from the chapel.

His right arm was bandaged—torn open by a bullet days before, but his rage kept him standing tall.

Emilio smirked through his bruises. "So this is what a king looks like when the throne is built on grief."

Alessio didn't answer. He simply turned and walked into the interrogation room. The walls were thick. Soundproof. The kind used for torturing ghosts.

They followed.

The Interrogation

The room was cold. Just one chair. One bulb swinging above them, casting dizzy shadows.

Emilio sat with the slow grace of a dying god. "You think this changes anything?" he rasped, eyes scanning the room like he'd memorized it once upon a time.

"Wars don't end with truth. They end when everyone's too dead to remember who started them."

Alessio didn't pace. He watched.

"I didn't kill her," Emilio said first. "Not directly. I'm not some amateur with a grudge and a knife. I orchestrated it. Hired the man. Paid him double to make it look like an accident."

Alessio's silence cracked. "Why?"

Emilio leaned back, expression devoid of shame. "Because your father wouldn't listen. Because your mother had influence. Because nothing breeds loyalty in a Moretti like a funeral."

There was a tremor in Emilio's voice then—not regret. Nostalgia.

"I needed your father to react. Emotionally. Recklessly. He always prided himself on control. So I broke it. Your mother was the only soft spot he had left. I exploited it."

Alessio clenched his fists. "She wasn't part of your war."

"She was married to power. That made her fair game."

A beat of silence. Then Emilio added, with casual cruelty, "And she wasn't alone."

Alessio stilled.

Emilio's lips curled. "Isabella's mother knew."

Isabella was twelve when she first saw her mother cry. Not over death. Not over love. But over a name whispered in the hallway.

"Moretti," her mother had said, eyes rimmed in red, hands trembling as she tucked a rosary under her pillow. "Some sins aren't forgiven. Some are passed down."

Back then, Isabella didn't understand.

Now, she remembered everything.

The Veil Lifts

Alessio said nothing. Not even a breath escaped.

Emilio continued, satisfied with the wound he'd opened.

"She helped me cover it. She burned documents. Redirected suspicion. All to protect her daughter. You think Isabella's innocent? Her bloodline was built on sacrifice too. Just quieter."

"You're lying," Alessio growled.

"Am I?" Emilio leaned forward. "Ask her what she found in her mother's jewelry box the night before your wedding was announced."

She had gone searching for earrings.

What she found was a sealed envelope tucked inside velvet—charred at the edges. Inside: a photograph of Alessio's mother. Smiling. Holding Isabella as a baby.

And on the back, her mother's handwriting:
"Forgive me for what I let happen. This was the price."

Isabella had burned the letter. Not to destroy evidence—but to unsee a truth she couldn't bear.

Alessio's hand slammed the table. "You expect me to believe Isabella knew all this?"

Emilio laughed. "She knows pieces. Enough to unravel her."

The door opened behind them. Isabella entered, silent as breath, but her eyes were oceans of storm.

"You bastard," she whispered.

"I gave you everything," Emilio said, almost fondly. "Even the man you'll end up destroying."

"Don't speak like you know me."

He smiled, teeth stained with blood. "I made you."

Alessio stood between them like a wall. "Leave."

"No," Isabella whispered, stepping closer. "He wants to die with power in his mouth. I want to take it from him first."

A Daughter's Goodbye

She stepped into the room like a ghost that refused to stay buried.

Her heels clicked softly on the concrete, a delicate sound that echoed louder than screams in a space like this.

Her eyes swept over her father, chained and bleeding, but her expression didn't falter. No tears. No tremble. Just silence—weaponized.

Emilio looked up at her with a smile too calm for a man who knew his fate had been sealed.

"There she is," he said, like it was a reunion. "My masterpiece."

Isabella didn't speak. Not at first. She moved slowly, deliberately, each step echoing a memory—a funeral, a secret, a scar.

"You always told me I had your eyes," she said softly, stopping just inches away.

"But now I see it was the only thing you didn't twist into something unrecognizable."

Emilio cocked his head. "I gave you more than eyes, sweetheart. I gave you the instincts to survive. To see weakness before it strikes. That's what's kept you alive this long, isn't it? Not your mother's prayers. My blood."

She laughed—a sound so cold it froze the room.

"Your blood is poison," she said.

"And you spent your life dripping it into my veins, calling it protection."

Emilio leaned forward, lips cracked but smirking. "You say that now. But when they came for you—when they surrounded you like wolves—I was the one who taught you how to bare your teeth."

Isabella's gaze flickered, just briefly, and in that moment her grief nearly cracked through.

"You didn't teach me how to survive," she said. "You taught me how to erase myself."

She crouched then—eye level now, nose inches from his—and her voice dropped to a whisper that sliced bone.

"Do you remember my cousin Luca?" she asked. "The one who vanished the day after he confronted you about a ledger?"

Emilio didn't flinch. But his pupils dilated—just enough.

"I know what you did to him. He wasn't your first secret. Just your sloppiest."

Her hands curled into fists, nails cutting skin. But she didn't raise them. No violence. Just words. Words that hurt more.

"You murdered someone I loved because he got too close to the truth," she said. "And you think I'll weep for you now?"

She stood up slowly.

"I'm not your daughter anymore. I buried her the moment I realized you built my future with a lie in every brick."

She turned to Alessio, voice steady now.

"We're done."

And without waiting for permission or forgiveness, she walked out, leaving the door open behind her like an invitation to hell.

Alessio remained.

The light above flickered, catching the edges of his scars like glints of steel.

He hadn't spoken since Isabella left, hadn't moved except to crack his knuckles once—slowly, rhythmically—like a man winding up for something he wasn't sure he'd survive.

"You really think this ends with you?" he said, finally.

Emilio blinked once, slowly. "No. It ends with her."

Alessio's eyes narrowed.

"You've built your whole life trying to control women you couldn't understand," he said. "Isabella, her mother, my mother… You kill what you can't predict."

"And what would you have done?" Emilio rasped. "You think you're different?"

"I'm not," Alessio said without hesitation. "But I know the difference between a wound and a weakness. You mistook one for the other—and it made you reckless."

He stepped forward, close enough now that the stench of dried blood, sweat, and rot filled his lungs. But he didn't recoil.

"You think you're the center of the story," Alessio said. "But the truth is, you're just the rot beneath the roots."

Emilio's smile returned, faint now. Tired.

"Rot makes the soil fertile," he said. "It breeds new life."

Alessio leaned in.

"And sometimes… it needs to be burned."

As he turned to leave, Emilio's voice rasped from behind like the final hiss of a dying serpent.

"You think you know your monsters…"

Alessio stopped, half in shadow.

"…but what if your mother fed them too?"

The words lingered—low, venom-laced, soaked in implication. Not a threat. A revelation. A curse.

Alessio didn't turn. Didn't respond.

But the silence he left behind was loud enough to bury a thousand sins.

CHAPTER 29

- Ruins of the Heart -

GRIEF DIDN'T KNOCK anymore , it lived in her now. It haunted her reflection, curled in the corners of her eyes, stretched behind every exhausted breath.

The woman staring back at her in the mirror looked like someone halfway undone—mascara smudged like warpaint, lips bitten raw, bruises blooming like violets across her collarbone.

But it wasn't the bruises that made her look like a ghost.

It was the way her mother's shadow clung to her.

She could see it now, in brutal hindsight. The patterns. The silences. The things they both swallowed instead of screaming.

Her mother had been polished obedience wrapped around a storm—and now, Isabella realized, so was she.

They'd both loved men too dangerous to love. Both played roles they didn't write. Both silenced truth for the illusion of control.

I became her the day I kept his secrets, Isabella thought.

The weight of that truth crushed her chest like stone.

She curled up on the edge of the bed—no sheets, no warmth, just her own trembling hands and a heart unraveling by the minute.

Her fingers clutched the locket around her neck. It held nothing. No picture. Just memory. And guilt.

Had she ever made a choice for herself?
Or had she always been a pawn in someone else's war?

First her father. Then Emilio. Now Alessio.

Or maybe, she thought bitterly, *she'd never been a queen. Just a prettier knife.*

The door opened behind her.

She didn't move. Didn't flinch. But the ache in her spine knew it was him.

Alessio walked in like a man bearing his own funeral. His coat was wet, his eyes darker than she'd ever seen them—like a storm that forgot how to end.

"I told him I wouldn't kill him," he said quietly. "Because I wanted you to be free of him. Not just from his breath or his reach—but from the grip he still had on your soul."

She closed her eyes.

"I don't know who I am anymore," she whispered.

Alessio crossed the room slowly. He knelt beside her, like she was something sacred he didn't dare touch without permission.

"Then let me remind you," he said.

His hand found hers—scarred meeting scarred—and it was enough to make her shatter.

"I should hate you," she whispered, broken.

"I'd let you," he murmured. "If it meant you could breathe again."

She turned her face to him, lips trembling.

"I thought I was built from loyalty," she said. "But it turns out,

I'm made of grief."

He touched her cheek, reverent.

"Then let me grieve with you."

Holy Kind of Desperation

It didn't start with hunger.

It started with silence.

A quiet understanding that this might be the last moment they could touch each other without blood between them.

The war hadn't stopped—it had only paused long enough to let them fall.

Alessio undressed her slowly. Not like a man stripping a woman—but like a mourner unwrapping a relic. Like he knew every inch of her was a battlefield and he was stepping into the fire willingly.

She let him.

When his lips met hers, there was no dominance, no command. Only surrender. His mouth moved like prayer, and his hands shook—not from lust, but from reverence.

He didn't claim her body.

He worshipped her ruin.

Every kiss was penance. Every breath was borrowed from a version of the future they knew they might never see. His mouth trailed down her neck, over her shoulder, slow and trembling.

She gasped—not from pleasure, but from the unbearable gentleness of it all.

When he entered her, it wasn't fast or fierce.

It was slow. Painfully slow.

Like they were carving love into grief. Like they were learning how to live inside a dying moment.

She clung to him like salvation, nails raking down his back, breath caught in her throat. His name was a cry and a curse. He whispered hers like he was bleeding it.

And when she came apart beneath him, she wasn't just moaning—she was weeping.

It felt like redemption.
Like maybe, just maybe, love could survive the wreckage.

They lay tangled in silence afterward. Skin slick. Breaths ragged.

Isabella curled into him, tracing the scar on his chest—the one Emilio gave him. Her finger paused over it like it was a wound she could rewrite.

"Do you still trust me?" she asked.

He didn't answer immediately.

Instead, he pulled her tighter.

"I don't trust anything anymore," he whispered. "But I still love you."

The words hit harder than any bullet. Because love, without trust, was a kind of agony she'd never learned how to survive.

But neither of them pulled away.

Because even in ruin, they belonged here—in this wreckage they made with their own hands.

She lifted her head, eyes burning.

"If we burn," she whispered, "we burn together."

Alessio didn't answer.

He just kissed her again—slow, wrecked, and holy.

Like they were already on fire.

CHAPTER 30

- The Blood Pact -

THE AIR INSIDE THE Moretti estate stank of gun oil, cigars, and old betrayal.

Alessio sat at the head of the table—the chair once carved for his father, the throne of a dynasty now soaked in blood. Around him, remnants of two families circled like vultures dressed in silk:

Moretti defectors, Romano loyalists, silent soldiers still unsure which crest they served.

He didn't blame them. In this new war, loyalty was a relic.

He scanned the room and saw ghosts sitting between the living. Marco. Emilio. His mother. Hers.

The sins of the past stared back at him with empty eyes.

But it was Isabella who broke the silence.

She stood at his side—not behind him, never behind—and when she spoke, her voice was neither bride nor daughter. It was forged iron.

"Enough blood has been spilled for men who are now dead. The ones standing here? We're either the future… or the next names carved into tombstones."

She let that sit like a gun cocking.

"We're not asking you to trust us," she continued. "We're asking you to choose who you want to bleed beside when the final war begins."

There were no cheers. No raised glasses.

Just silence.

Then Enzo Romano, an uncle she once feared, stepped forward.

And he nodded.

"We follow you now. Both of you."

The pact was born in silence. The kind that comes right before a storm.

They burned the old banners that night.

Romano red. Moretti gold.

They tossed them into a steel barrel behind the estate, watched silk twist in flame until the sky smelled like ash and defiance. Isabella didn't flinch as the fire rose. She let the heat lick her skin, unbothered by the sparks that kissed her collarbone.

She was done playing innocent. Done pretending there was a way out that didn't demand sacrifice.

Alessio stood beside her, arms folded, gaze hard. They hadn't spoken since the truce had been sealed. Not in words, anyway.

Their silence now wasn't cold. It was charged. Alive.

"You think we're doing the right thing?" she finally asked, staring into the burning crest of her family name.

"I don't know what right means anymore," he said. "But I know I'm doing it with you."

She turned toward him, slow, the flickering light casting him in shadow and flame. He looked like a god sculpted in vengeance.

And yet, when he looked at her, she felt soft again. Not weak. Soft in the way mountains are soft before an avalanche.

They had chosen ruin.

Now they had to survive it.

The Pact Made in Blood

The ring wasn't made of gold.

It was iron. Cold and dark and ancient. Forged from the melted bullets fired the night Marco died. Symbolic. Ugly. Real.

Alessio held it between two fingers, watching it catch the dim light of their war room.

"No priest. No veil," he murmured. "Just this."

Isabella reached for it, her fingers brushing his. "No promises," she added, "that we can't keep."

He slid it onto her finger—not with grace, but with reverence. A soldier's offering. A sinner's devotion.

Then she pressed a blade to her palm. Shallow. Clean. A crimson pearl bloomed.

He did the same.

And when their blood touched, it wasn't ceremonial.

It was final.

A new kind of vow—sealed not in God's name, but in vengeance.

They didn't kiss. Not yet. They simply stood there, their joined hands dripping red onto the marble, their breathing matched like a lullaby sung to fire.

The blood pooled at their feet.

A pact made not for peace—but for war.

The calm before a war is the most dangerous kind. It tempts

you to hope.

For Alessio, it came in the way Isabella brushed her fingers through his hair as he sat at the edge of the bed, scars and sins heavy on his spine.

For Isabella, it came in the way he looked at her in candlelight, not like she was a weapon—but like she was the last light before darkness swallowed them whole.

"We don't get forever," he whispered into her shoulder. "But we get this."

She nodded, lips against his neck.

"I'll take this. And every second they didn't want us to have."

Outside, the city buzzed with something electric—gunmetal tension, whispered allegiances, footsteps that didn't belong to either of them.

War was coming.

But tonight… they were still breathing.

Still side by side.

Still *theirs*.

No priest. No vows. Just blood.

That was their love story.

CHAPTER 31

- House of Fire -

THE AIR WAS thick with sulfur and anticipation. Alessio stood at the edge of the forest, staring down at the Romano compound like a god about to unleash wrath.

The estate, once a monument to opulence, now looked like a mausoleum—its lights flickering, guards pacing like shadows waiting for absolution.

He breathed in.

Not for courage. He didn't believe in that anymore.

This war wasn't about courage.

It was about *closure*.

He turned to the men behind him. Former Romano soldiers, exiled Morettis. Enemies made allies through blood and necessity. There were no banners, no oaths. Just bullets and names carved into revenge.

"Tonight," he said, voice low and clean, "we don't fight for a family. We fight to finish what they started."

They moved on silent feet. Ghosts in the dark. And when the first shot rang out, it wasn't a warning.

It was a promise kept.

He had locked the door himself.

Left her inside the reinforced panic room beneath the Moretti wine cellar. She screamed at him as the vault door sealed—hit him in the chest, cursed his name like a woman betrayed.

But he saw the fear in her eyes. And that's what terrified him more than bullets.

She wasn't afraid to die.

She was afraid *he* would.

So he lied.

"This isn't your fight," he'd said.

A laugh, bitter as poison. "It's always been my fight, Alessio."

But he turned the lock anyway.

And now, as he stepped over the blood of men who'd once been uncles and cousins, he prayed she'd stay locked away—safe from the carnage.

He didn't know yet that she had already escaped.

That the queen had broken her own chains.

The estate was burning from the inside out.

Molotovs shattered through stained glass windows. Explosions lit the Romanos' ancestral halls like candles for the dead. Screams pierced the night, mixing with the scent of gunpowder and betrayal.

Alessio moved through it all like a storm in a tailored suit—blood on his collar, fury in his hands. Every shot was a name. Every body, a retribution.

He found Marco in the ballroom. The same room where a fake wedding had nearly ended everything. Ironic.

The man was cornered, bleeding from a shoulder wound, wild-eyed and panting.

"You were always weaker than me," Marco spat, dragging

himself to his feet. "She'll bury you like she buried me."

Alessio didn't speak.

He aimed.

Fired.

Once through the chest. Once through the head.

Not mercy. *Closure.*

And the war cracked open like a dying star.

He didn't see her at first.

Through the haze, through the blood, through the dying groans of a war's final breath—he didn't see her.

But then—A scream. A gunshot.

And there she was.

Isabella.

Smoke in her hair, fire in her eyes, blood on her silk blouse. She held a pistol like a prophecy and moved through the ruin like a goddess draped in vengeance.

"You locked me in," she said when their eyes met across the flames.

"I know."

"You should've known better."

And despite everything—the war, the ash, the death still clinging to the walls—he smiled.

Because she had come for him.

Not as a savior.

But as an equal.

Letter in the Pocket

It was strange—how something as small as paper could feel

heavier than a weapon.

The letter had been hidden beneath the inner lining of Alessio's black suit jacket, stitched so seamlessly that even he hadn't noticed it until the fabric tore as he dodged a bullet behind the shattered pillar of the west wing.

Blood dripped from his temple, and his breath came ragged. But his fingers, almost guided by something unseen, reached into the torn seam—and found it.

A single folded page. Yellowed slightly. Creased at the corners. Ink faded but legible. The handwriting was unmistakable—his father's. He hadn't seen it in over a decade, not since the man's death at the hands of the Romanos had cemented Alessio's path in blood.

His vision blurred—not from smoke, but memory.

The war screamed around him. Men shouted, gunfire cracked like thunder, and the house burned down to its bones. But in that moment, none of it mattered. The world narrowed to ink and parchment.

He unfolded it.

Alessio,

If you're reading this, then I'm gone—and not just in body.
The weight of this family will try to break you. It broke me in ways I never showed.

You'll want vengeance. I did too. Every bone in my body begged for it. But vengeance doesn't build legacies. It buries them.

You're not like me. You never were. You love harder. You feel deeper. That will be your greatest weapon... and your greatest wound.

So when the time comes, don't choose wrath.
Choose her.

Even if it kills you.

—Your father, Matteo Moretti.

His hands trembled.

Not from fear.

But from the realization that his father—so cold in life, so rigid in power—had known this moment would come. That Alessio would be forced to choose not between winning and losing, but between surviving and *living*.

He folded the letter with reverence, slipping it back inside his jacket, close to his heart—closer than any weapon he'd ever carried.

And then he turned to the fire.

To the choice.

To her.

It wasn't the sound of gunfire that led them.

It was silence.

A silence so sharp it sliced through the chaos like a knife through silk.

Alessio and Isabella moved through the crumbling corridor of the old Romano cellar—his gun drawn, her steps a whisper behind him.

Flames danced along the cracked ceiling, casting long shadows that made the walls appear as if they wept black tears.

There it was—the last door.

Iron-bound. Ancient. Hidden beneath the floorboards of a wine rack destroyed by shrapnel. The kind of door built not to keep people out, but to keep monsters in.

He didn't hesitate.

Alessio kicked it open with a force that shook the hinges. Smoke coiled down into the dark like a serpent fleeing light.

The passage beyond descended into the earth—narrow and suffocating, lined with old brick and dripping pipes. A forgotten tunnel, likely built for smuggling during Prohibition, now used for escape.

Cowards' bones lined paths like these.

And that's where they found him.

Emilio.

Running.

The man looked over his shoulder, eyes wild, face bruised and bloody. He didn't pause. Didn't speak. He just kept running.

Down. Deeper. Into darkness.

Isabella stepped forward, gun raised—but Alessio held out a hand.

"No."

She blinked. "Why?"

"Because death down there would be too kind."

She lowered her weapon, breath shallow. And in that moment, he could feel it between them—the understanding. The rage they shared had hollowed them, but it hadn't claimed them. Not completely.

They let him flee.

The fire would find him eventually.

Or his guilt would.

Whichever came first.

Alessio turned back, fingers brushing Isabella's as they ascended from the cellar of ghosts.

They didn't need to chase monsters anymore.

They had already *become* the storm.

He stepped through the war's ashes with her at his side, their hands bloodied but joined.

He walked into the flames not to end a war…

…but to save the only thing worth dying for.

Not a family not a name, but *her*.

Always her.

CHAPTER 32

- The Last Bullet -

THE COMPOUND SMELLED of smoke, sweat, and old betrayal. Not the fresh kind that stung like a slap, but the kind that festered for years—slow, deliberate. The kind that shaped you before you knew it had touched you.

Isabella moved through the scorched hallways like a ghost in her own skin. Her boots crunched over glass and blackened tile.

Her grip on the pistol never wavered, but her pulse roared like thunder in her ears.

She knew where he'd be.

Rats always fled to the bones of the house.

A locked wine chamber below the east wing—Emilio's old sanctuary. One of the few places untouched by the recent fire, almost as if the flames refused to touch the last of the devils.

She found him sitting at a table covered in dust and maps, bruised, bloodied, but not afraid.

Never afraid.

"Belladonna," he rasped, smiling like a man who'd already won.

"I knew you'd come."

She raised the gun.

He didn't flinch.

The Poisoned Truth

"You don't have to do this," Emilio said, voice low, almost tender. "Not once you know."

Isabella didn't speak.

"You think you were a pawn," he continued. "But you were the catalyst. The real reason everything burned."

She gritted her teeth. "Shut up."

"Your mother lied to you. Lied to all of us."
He reached into his jacket—slowly, carefully—and pulled out a folded document, yellowed with time.

Isabella didn't lower the gun, but she took the paper with her free hand.

Birth certificate. Handwritten note. Hospital files.

Then the words that changed everything:

Father: Emilio Romano.
Mother: Luciana Romano.

She couldn't breathe.

"You're lying," she whispered.

"I wish I were," Emilio murmured. "But your blood isn't Moretti. Not fully. You were born from betrayal. Conceived in a moment your mother never forgave herself for. She raised you in lies to protect her legacy—and to keep you from me."

He took a step forward.

"You don't have to pull that trigger. We can disappear. Start something new. No one has to know what you are."

Tears burned in her throat, but none fell. Her finger hovered on the trigger.

And that's when she heard the footsteps behind her.

Alessio.

He hadn't meant to hear it.

Hadn't wanted to.

But fate, cruel and unrelenting, had dragged him here—right at the edge of the old world unraveling.

He stepped into the room silently, his gun already drawn, his eyes on her, not Emilio.

Isabella.

The woman who had shattered him and saved him all in one breath.

His heart pounded.

Would she pull the trigger?
Would she hesitate?
Was blood thicker than love—or just heavier?

The air was thick with smoke and legacy.

She didn't look back. But she knew he was there.

She lowered the gun.

And his chest cracked in two.

But then—

She lifted it again. Higher this time. Aimed directly at Emilio's forehead.

And pulled the trigger.

The Last Bullet

The shot echoed like a funeral bell.

Emilio's body jerked once, then crumpled backward into the chair, eyes wide in death. No last words. No redemption. Just silence, swift and absolute.

Isabella stood frozen, the pistol still raised, smoke rising from the barrel like incense from a dying altar.

She whispered, voice hoarse but clear:

"Blood made me. But love made me choose."

Then her legs buckled.

Alessio caught her before she hit the floor, arms wrapping around her trembling frame as the ceiling groaned above them.

Dust rained from the rafters. Flames licked the edges of the room as if the fire itself had waited for this ending.

He held her to his chest, her face pressed into his neck, her body wracked with shivers. Not from fear. Not from weakness.

From the cost of survival.

They barely made it out before the structure began to collapse behind them.

The fire wasn't just physical. It was *symbolic.* The crumbling house, the legacy of lies, the empire built on blood—it was all being reduced to ash.

Outside, the dawn cracked open above the horizon, a brutal slash of red across the sky.

They didn't speak for a long time.

Alessio sat on the gravel beside the compound's crumbling gate, Isabella curled in his lap, wrapped in his jacket.

Her eyes were red. His hands were still shaking.

But they were alive.

Together.

"What now?" she asked eventually, her voice small.

Alessio didn't answer right away. He kissed her temple. Then her cheek. Then her lips—soft, slow, reverent.

As if she were the only thing anchoring him to this world.

In a room full of smoke and corpses, he kissed her like it was the only thing keeping them alive.

Because maybe… it was.

CHAPTER 33

- After the War -

THE VILLA STOOD ON a cliffside just beyond Trapani, where the sea kissed the sky and time forgot how to move forward. No guards patrolled the perimeter.

No cameras, no guns, no orders barked into radios.

Only olive trees swaying gently in the breeze and the occasional hum of bees kissing lemon blossoms.

It didn't feel like exile. It felt like choosing peace—for once.

Isabella had learned to let the silence fill her bones, not break them. She rose with the sun and fed stray cats that had made the ruins of an old chapel their kingdom.

She drank bitter espresso on the terrace and watched Alessio argue with his vines like they were disobedient soldiers.

He'd named the vineyard *La Casa delle Secondi Occasioni—The House of Second Chances.*

The irony didn't escape her.

Neither of them had known what life would be like after the fire. After the bullet. After the blood-soaked ending of the world they'd once ruled.

But this?

This was something sacred.

Isabella didn't tell anyone her real name anymore.

To the women who walked through the glass doors of her trauma foundation in Palermo, she was *Dott.ssa Ilaria Ventresca*.

She wore soft sweaters and matte lipstick and never raised her voice. They never asked about her past, and she never offered it.

But every scar she treated, every hand she held, every broken girl who walked out standing a little straighter—each one was her redemption.

She worked in silence. In softness. In absolute contrast to the inferno she'd survived.

But every night, when she came home, the weight of her past settled beside her like a shadow she no longer feared.

She'd made peace with her ghosts. Most days.

Some nights, she still woke gasping.

Some nights, Alessio would be there before her breath returned, holding her like he'd held her in the ashes.

Olive Trees and Unspoken Promises

It was the olive trees that gave it away.

One evening, she found him standing beneath their branches, shirt stained with earth, hair tousled by the wind, a small velvet box in his dirt-covered hand.

There was no speech. No kneeling.

Just him.

And the kind of stillness that said everything loud.

He opened the box.

Inside, a simple silver ring glinted against black velvet.

No rubies. No blood.

Just silver. Clean. Untouched.

She looked down at the band she still wore—the one forged in the blood pact. Sharp-edged. Heavy with memory.

"This one," Alessio said softly, "isn't for war."

She stared at it, heart threatening to tremble out of her chest. "Are you asking me to marry you?"

"No." His voice dropped, dark and quiet. "I'm asking if I can be yours without needing to survive a war to earn it."

She didn't cry.

But her hands shook as she slid the blood-ring off... and slipped the silver one on.

And when he kissed her knuckles, it wasn't for show or claim or ceremony.

It was worship.

They said their vows with no witnesses.

No priest.

Just two souls beneath a Sicilian sky darker than ink, the sea roaring below like applause from forgotten gods.

He whispered, "Ti scelgo, sempre."
I choose you, always.

She whispered back, "Anche se brucia."
Even if it burns.

And that was all they needed.

"Do you ever miss it?" she asked.
"The war?"

He kissed her hand. "No. But I'd start another one if it meant keeping you."

And beneath the dark Sicilian sky,
with blood on their past and hope in their hands,
they wrote the only vow they ever needed:

Survive. Together.

The End

AFTERWORD

This story was never about a mafia empire.

Not really.

It was about two people born in blood, raised in ruin, and chained to legacies they never asked to inherit. Alessio Moretti and Isabella Romano were always destined to collide—not just as enemies or lovers, but as two fractured souls searching for a reason to live beyond revenge.

Forbidden Hearts is a love story, yes. But it's also a survival story.

It's about choosing tenderness in a world that teaches violence. It's about defiance—the quiet kind that doesn't scream but stays. It's about the courage it takes to break cycles passed down like heirlooms, and the impossible beauty of choosing love, even when it costs everything.

Throughout the pages, I wrote about fire. Burning kingdoms. Burning vows. Burning pride. But in the end, what remains in the ash is always the same:

Hope.

If you've made it here—thank you. Truly. You carried Isabella and Alessio through war, grief, lust, betrayal, and the kind of redemption that doesn't come wrapped in perfection but in pain, forgiveness, and the promise of something better.

Maybe you saw yourself in Isabella's defiance or Alessio's guarded heart. Maybe you needed to believe that even in the darkest corners of the world, love can still bloom.

If so—this story was for you.

And remember this:

You don't have to come from light to deserve it.

With fire and love,

Nolan Crest

ABOUT THE AUTHOR

Nolan Crest

Nolan Crest writes stories with blood under their fingernails and poetry stitched between their pages. Known for crafting dark, emotionally charged romances that walk the line between ruin and redemption, Nolan explores the raw, haunting beauty of love born in impossible places.

With a background in psychology and an obsession with morally gray characters, Nolan weaves narratives where power and passion collide—where hearts don't just fall, they shatter and rebuild.

When not writing, Nolan can be found drinking black coffee at midnight, researching crime families like it's a love language, or whispering plot twists to the sea.

Forbidden Hearts is the first in a universe of stories that ask: What if your soulmate is also your greatest undoing?

BOOKS IN THIS SERIES

Forbidden Desires

Forbidden Lust

Forbidden Vows

BOOKS BY THIS AUTHOR

Reckless Love

Craving Love

Untamed Passion

Wild Obsession

Irresistible Heat

The Sorcerer's Kiss

Bound By Midnight